A

'So—no man in your life, then?' he asked, just to be sure, and she chuckled ruefully.

'Are you kidding? Who'd put up with this?'

'I would,' he said quietly, after a heartbeat, and her eyes widened. 'I'm divorced. I've got four kids who've been gutted by their mother's defection. There's no way on God's green earth I'll ever remarry and put my kids or myself in a position where we can be hurt like that again, but I'm lonely. I don't have a social life either, and I don't have time for one. I don't have time for someone who expects me to be home at a set time and free at the weekends and available to host dinner parties. But I...'

'Have needs?' she said softly.

He swallowed hard. 'Oh, yes. I have needs. All sorts of needs. Not just physical, but...'

She smiled. 'Me, too.' And without another word, she reached up on tiptoe, slid her arms around his neck and touched her lips to his.

Caroline Anderson has the mind of a butterfly. She's been a nurse, a secretary, a teacher, run her own soft-furnishing business and now she's settled on writing. She says, 'I was looking for that elusive something. I finally realised it was variety, and now I have it in abundance. Every book brings new horizons and new friends, and in between books I have learned to be a juggler. My teacher husband John and I have two beautiful and talented daughters, Sarah and Hannah, umpteen pets and several acres of Suffolk that nature tries to reclaim every time we turn our backs!' Caroline also writes for the Mills & Boon® Tender Romance™ series.

Recent titles by the same author:

THE BABY FROM NOWHERE
  (Medical Romance™)
THE PREGNANT TYCOON
  (Tender Romance™)
FOR CHRISTMAS, FOR ALWAYS
  (Medical Romance™)
THE BABY BONDING
  (Medical Romance™)
WITH THIS BABY...
  (Tender Romance™)

ASSIGNMENT: CHRISTMAS

BY
CAROLINE ANDERSON

MILLS & BOON®

*First published in Great Britain 2004
Large Print edition 2005
Harlequin Mills & Boon Limited,
Eton House, 18-24 Paradise Road,
Richmond, Surrey TW9 1SR*

© Caroline Anderson 2004

ISBN 0 263 18463 3

*Set in Times Roman 16½ on 18½ pt.
17-0605-49500*

*Printed and bound in Great Britain
by Antony Rowe Ltd, Chippenham, Wiltshire*

CHAPTER ONE

HE STROLLED in as if he owned the place.

Fliss had a scant thirty seconds to study him as he checked out the department, his eyes tracking over it in a way that made her glad they'd had time to get it straight after the mayhem of the past few hours, and she enjoyed every one of those seconds.

The man was to die for. The fact that she should be finding out what he was doing here instead of gazing at him like a star-struck adolescent was quite beside the point.

He was fascinating. That lean and deceptively relaxed body, the clean-cut line of his jaw, the dark hair tousled by the fresh spring breeze and liberally threaded with grey—stuff the paperwork, she thought. This merits some *serious* study!

Perching on the edge of the tall chair, she indulged herself and ran her eyes over him

5

again. Hmm. About thirty-five, or maybe slightly older, she decided, but definitely in his prime. Oh, yes.

He was dressed in a casual shirt and trousers, a jacket slung over his shoulder on one finger, and he looked too alive, too vital to be indoors. She could picture him on a hillside, the wind tugging at his hair, his body braced against the elements.

He must be lost, she thought, because he certainly didn't belong here. Lost or looking for a relative. A wife, maybe. Lucky woman.

She wondered what he did for a living. Nothing sedentary, that was for sure. Something physical and active, if not for his occupation, then as a very serious hobby. Mountaineering? Rock-climbing? Or maybe just walking, striding hour after hour over wild and rugged heathland, at one with his surroundings.

And then his eyes locked with hers, and her heart jammed in her throat and cut off her airway. One side of his mouth kicked up slightly, and when he changed direction and started to move towards her, she couldn't have moved if her life had depended on it.

Move? She couldn't even breathe!

Tall and broad, with a long, effortless stride that ate up the floor and brought him right to her desk before she had time to say 'Hallelujah!', he positioned himself just *there* in front of her and scanned her with his eyes.

Gorgeous eyes. Smoky grey eyes, with laughter lines crinkling the outer corners and dead straight long black lashes that a lesser woman would kill for. She'd settle for simply looking at them.

Simply being the operative word.

That fleeting, crooked smile quirked his lips, but despite his casual demeanour, she just knew he hadn't missed a thing with that single sweeping glance. The department might look OK, but that was more than could be said of her! Her cheeks were flushed, her face bare of make-up because today had got off to a typi-cally chaotic start after a totally lousy yester-day, and she could feel her hair sliding out of the clip she'd hastily crammed it into and making a bid for freedom.

Rather like her brain.

Great first impression, she thought, and gave an inward groan. Knowing her luck he wouldn't be a lost mountaineer or a relative at all, but an inspector from some government department come to check them all out and find them wanting. Terrific. Well, at least she was making it easy for him!

The piercing grey eyes locked onto hers and held. 'You must be Felicity.'

Dear God, that voice. Like mocha, hot and dark and sinful, it made her heart jiggle about again just when it had settled down. Wasted on an inspector, she thought, at the same time realising that if he knew her name, he hadn't just strolled in by accident but must be there for a purpose.

Which made the inspector thing more likely, unfortunately.

She nearly got to her feet, then thought better of it. The way her body was misbehaving, she'd probably fall flat on her face!

'I'm Felicity,' she confirmed, putting down her pen before she dropped it. 'Better known as Fliss, a.k.a. Sister Ryman, in charge of the department this afternoon, for my sins. What can I do for you?'

He held out his hand—the one that wasn't dangling the jacket over his shoulder—and the smile flickered briefly again and was gone. 'Tom Whittaker. Just thought I'd come in and familiarise myself with the department before tomorrow.'

Her first reaction was relief. The next was astonishment. This was their long-awaited and much discussed new A and E consultant? Funny how nobody had ever mentioned that he was so incredibly darned good-looking!

She slid off the edge of the tall chair and stood up, taking his hand in hers and instantly regretting her innate good manners, because that single, simple touch, that everyday social gesture, was enough to bring her to her knees.

She retrieved her hand and tried to remember how to smile. 'Welcome to the Audley Memorial,' she said, wondering if her voice, too, was going to desert her. 'You're lucky, it's been hell but it seems to have settled down—'

And right on cue, the phone rang just inches from her hand.

'Me and my big mouth,' she muttered. 'Excuse me.'

He chuckled, propped his lean, beautifully crafted body up against the desk and stood there just on the edge of her vision while she tried to concentrate.

Two seconds into the call was enough to have her full and undivided attention.

'RTA on the Ipswich road four miles south of Audley—five vehicles involved, multiple casualties. ETA ten minutes for the first crew, but there's an entrapment. There's a GP on site but he could do with some back-up. Any chance of a rapid response team?'

At the tail end of this grim weekend? They'd be thrilled. Fliss rolled her eyes. 'Sure. I'll get them to call you once they're under way. Any info on the others?'

'Not yet. I'll let you have it as soon as it comes through.'

'Right. I'll speak to you shortly.'

She returned the phone to its cradle and turned to their new consultant. 'Sorry, all hell's just about to break loose. We've got a multiple pile-up—'

'Want to take advantage of me?'

Her eyes flicked to his and she gave a short laugh. 'I'd love to, but I'm a bit busy at the moment,' she retorted, then headed for the staffroom, leaving her new colleague to follow if he would while she mentally kicked herself for her smart mouth. Then she heard him chuckle softly right behind her, and her breath eased out on a sigh of relief. Well, thank God he had a sense of humour. He'd need it in here.

She intercepted Meg. 'RTA coming in—can you clear the decks? It could be big.'

'Sure.'

She turned on her heel, and Fliss continued on to the staffroom where some of the team were grabbing a hasty but well-earned cup of tea.

'Sorry, guys, Rapid Response, please. Multiple RTA and an entrapment four miles south on the Ipswich road. Control have got the details. Who's going to draw the short straw?'

'I'll go,' Nick Baker said, getting up without hesitation.

'You just love to play with the flashing lights and the siren,' Sophie teased, following him up, and he arched a brow.

'So, are you coming, too?'

'Sure. Any excuse to get out of here. I'll get the stuff.'

And just like that they were gone, and Fliss turned to the others. 'First ambulance ETA about eight minutes now, no details, but can we get Resus ready and clear the decks for walking wounded? Five vehicles, but one of them could be a minibus, knowing our luck. Oh, and this is Tom Whittaker, our new consultant. Someone find him an apron or a set of scrubs, please. I'd hate to waste a useful body.'

She turned to him, one eyebrow raised. 'Assuming you meant what you said about taking advantage of you?'

Laughter lurked in his eyes, but his tone, when he spoke, was perfectly businesslike. 'Of course,' he said, deadpan. 'I'll need to make a phone call first.'

'Help yourself. I'll leave you to introduce yourself to everyone here as you need to. I have to go and talk to Reception and sort out who's doing triage—'

'I'll do it,' Meg offered, coming back from the cubicles. 'There's nobody urgent out here, so I've sent them back into the waiting room. There's a guy with a broken nail who's raising the roof, but he'll live.'

'Mr Cordy,' she said. 'I was just about to remove the nail and dress it. I was waiting for the local to work.'

'So he said—amongst other things. I'll go and get rid of the obvious malingerers, if you like.'

'Wonderful.'

She glanced at her watch, then at Tom's retreating back. One of the nurses was taking him towards the stores, her legs bustling to keep up with that long, lazy stride, and Fliss dragged her eyes off him and forced herself to concentrate.

So he was beautifully put together. Big deal. The way her rota worked she'd probably hardly ever clap eyes on him, so it was irrelevant—and if her heart kept misbehaving like this every time she saw him, it might be just as well for the sake of her health!

She scooped up the phone and asked the switchboard to page the key members of staff who were likely to be needed urgently, starting with an anaesthetist and putting Orthopaedics and a general surgical team well up the list.

In the background she could hear Meg's calm, quiet voice reasoning with Mr Cordy, who was complaining bitterly that nobody cared if he lived or died. Ten seconds later she heard Meg saying firmly, 'Mr Cordy, you've torn your nail! I'm sure it's sore, but it's far from fatal. If you want to wait, by all means do so, but it may well be morning before you're seen now.'

'But I've had a local anaesthetic! It'll wear off!'

'We'll give you another one later,' she promised. 'And look on the bright side, at least it doesn't hurt now.'

'Hmm. I'll go and get some fish and chips and come back,' he said grudgingly. 'And you'd better save my place. I'm not waiting any longer than I have to! If I'm not seen first after this lot, I'll register a complaint.'

'Please, feel free,' Meg said tartly, obviously at the end of her tether, and seconds later she swept past Fliss and Tom, eyes flashing, and disappeared into Resus.

Fliss bit her lips and looked up, to see their new man watching her, his mouth twitching.

'I do love the drama queens,' he said softly. 'They make it all worthwhile.'

'Are you talking about Meg, or Mr Cordy?' she asked, and he snorted.

'Cordy. If I'd been out there, I'd have ripped the nail off and stuck a plaster on it. In fact, I still might.'

'To be fair, it's a little more than a broken nail,' she said, wondering why she was defending the less than patient patient, but Tom just arched a sceptical, amused brow and smiled.

'It had better be,' he said, then added, his voice becoming lower, 'Right, Felicity, I'm all yours.'

Oh, I wish, she thought, but stifled the reaction instantly. There was no room in her life for a man—any man—and most particularly not a man like this who could have any woman he wanted. He probably went for the beautiful blondes—those immaculately turned-out leggy creatures who never forgot their make-up or turned up for work with plaster dust in their hair and paint under their nails.

Not that she did very often, and she always scrubbed her hands before she went on duty, but inevitably some paint escaped her notice, and plaster dust was a bit of a hazard in her line of work.

Her other line of work, she reminded herself as the wail of the sirens drew nearer, because first and foremost she was a nurse, and she wouldn't have had it any other way.

'Right, we're on,' she said, flashing him a smile and wondering if he realised just how darned gorgeous he was. Working alongside him was going to be a huge exercise in frustration, she knew, but the first ambulance was coming into view now, lights flashing, and worrying about him was suddenly way down her list.

He might have known this was going to happen. He should have just walked away, gone home to his family and told his new colleagues he'd see them in the morning, but he couldn't do it. He'd never been able to, and that, of course, had always been one of Jane's greatest grumbles.

His mother and father, bless them, had said they'd feed the kids and get them to bed, and he knew they meant it when they said they didn't mind, but he still felt a prickle of guilt.

He felt his lips press together in a grim line, and without a word he fell into step beside Felicity, his stride automatically adjusting to hers as she hurried to meet the ambulance.

The kids would be fine, and he knew his parents enjoyed the opportunity to spend time with them. He put them out of his mind and tried to concentrate on what Felicity was saying, and as they walked towards the doors he felt the familiar surge of adrenaline, the buzz he always felt when the pace picked up.

He loved working at the cutting edge, in the thick of it, never knowing what was coming in when those sirens wailed. That was why he worked in A and E, not surgery or general practice, and why he never walked away.

And he told himself firmly that his willingness to stay on and help had nothing—*nothing!*—to do with the teasing eyes, smart mouth and womanly curves of his new colleague!

He was amazing to work with. Fliss took him under her wing, and tried not to analyse her motives too closely. She'd thought she'd find him distracting, all that gorgeous man lined up next to her, but after the first few seconds of watching him work she forgot about everything except their patient.

A woman in her twenties or early thirties, she'd sustained serious chest and pelvic injuries and her blood pressure was dangerously low. One fumble, one moment of hesitation or indecision and she could be dead, Fliss realised, and she wondered how Tom would cope.

Brilliantly, was her answer. He had her assessed in no time flat, another line pouring fluids into her, and within minutes she had a chest drain in to relieve the pressure on her lungs from the tension pneumothorax, then he gently sprang her pelvis, making her moan with pain.

'It's gone,' he said. 'Right, let's have plates of the total spine, chest and pelvis to start with. Might as well know what we're dealing with here. Have we got an ex-fix kit available?'

Fliss nodded. 'Yes, but will you do that here rather than send her up to Theatre?'

'Would you want to be moved any further than necessary with an unstable pelvis?' he murmured softly. 'I know I wouldn't. We can do it here, it'll be fine. We'll get the pictures and put it on if we need to. In the meantime, let's get some bloods checked for FBC, U&E

and glucose, and cross-match for six units. Those ribs look a bit unstable, too, and if one of them shifts she could end up with a flail chest and a perforated lung, if she hasn't got one already. I want her stable and out of here to Theatre stat.'

As luck would have it, the plates revealed that her pelvis was definitely fractured on both sides as a result of the side impact in the accident, and needed stabilising before she could be moved to minimise any further damage. He bent over their patient, quietly and calmly explaining to her what they were going to do.

'It sounds scary, but it's the best option and it's not nearly as bad as it looks. You'll be much more comfortable once it's all rigid again.'

'I hope so,' she gasped weakly. 'It can't be worse.'

Within minutes the external fixator was attached to Tom's satisfaction, and she was on her way up to Theatre.

He stripped off his gloves and apron, stretched out his back and shot Fliss a crooked grin.

'Next?'

She found herself smiling back, any reservations she might have had long forgotten in the face of his very evident skill. 'I can hear sirens approaching again—if you're sure you've got time?'

'Of course. I've got more time than some of them have,' he said truthfully, his eyes flicking to where another team was finally admitting defeat after all attempts to resuscitate their patient had failed.

'Thank you,' she said, but he just shrugged.

'Don't thank me, it's my job.'

'Not today.'

'Every day,' he corrected, and how could she argue with his conviction when she shared it herself? She was no more capable of walking away than he was.

'Better go and meet the next ambulance, then,' she said with a smile, and so they moved on to the next casualty, and then the next, working their way steadily through them alongside the other teams in Resus, while her respect for him grew by the minute.

He didn't have to be here. He could have been at home, but he'd rolled up his sleeves and mucked in without a murmur. And in truth, she didn't know what they would have done without him, because his contribution was immeasurable.

Outside in the cubicles the less seriously injured patients were being treated and assessed by other members of the team, queuing for X-rays and waiting for casts to be applied and stitches to be inserted, but in Resus lives hung in the balance, and it needed all their skill to save them.

And he had skill in spades, she was starting to realise.

In there, surrounded by the blips and hisses of the machinery and the succinct, coded commands that were second nature to all of them, Fliss and Tom worked side by side on one casualty after another almost in silence, hip to hip, shoulder to shoulder, and as the minutes turned to hours she realised that they were both anticipating the other, working together in absolute harmony as if they'd been doing it for years.

The realisation stunned her a little. She'd never felt the power of such teamwork before, and she wondered if it was just a fluke. Probably. Too busy to worry about it, she put it out of her mind and simply took advantage of their effortless silent communication to work even more efficiently, until the last of their patients were despatched to Theatre and they could finally stop.

'Well, that's it,' she said, stripping off her gloves and tilting her head to meet Tom's eyes, her usual friendly smile at the ready. But something happened in that moment, something elemental and outside all her experience, and as their eyes locked and held, the smile died on her lips.

And Fliss, who'd always thought she was an open book, suddenly realised that there were pages here that no one had ever seen before, and this man, this stranger with whom she'd worked so intuitively, was turning those pages with his all-seeing eyes, scanning her innermost thoughts and dreams, reading her fears, understanding her in a way not even she understood herself.

But it wasn't one-sided. She could see loneliness and sorrow there in his eyes, and need there, too, a need that was surely mirrored in her own, clear for him to see.

She realised she'd always held just a tiny bit of herself back, but in the short space of the last few hours a total stranger had connected in some instinctive and elemental way with that hidden part of her, and Fliss found the sudden bond forged between them slightly shocking.

Shocking and strangely exciting.

Evidently she wasn't alone. His eyes darkened, but then he seemed to come to his senses. A frown pleating his brow, he sucked in his breath and took a step back, breaking the bond and freeing her, to her relief and regret. She turned away, hot colour burning her cheeks, and busied herself clearing up the devastation while she dragged air into her lungs and tried to gather her thoughts.

Meg stopped her.

'Come on, it's time we went. Let the night staff clear up. It's after nine, we should have gone an hour ago, and you were ill yesterday. You need to rest, and you,' she added, turning to Tom, 'shouldn't be here at all.'

'What about Mr Cordy and his nail? Should I just do him first?' Fliss asked, concerned for her abandoned patient, but Meg just laughed.

'Oh, he got bored hours ago. He took a deep breath, pulled the nail off and asked for a plaster. He was out of here in three minutes.'

They laughed, but Tom's laughter sounded strained to her ears. How she could tell that when she'd known him such a short time she had no idea, but she could, just as she could tell that he regretted that brief, unguarded moment of intimacy, that soul-baring connection between them that had shaken the foundations of her world.

His, too, she realised in amazement, and wondered where they'd go from here.

He scrubbed a hand through his hair and smiled vaguely at them both, his next words answering her unspoken question. 'I'd better be getting back while I still have a family to speak to,' he said with forced cheer, and Fliss, hearing the word 'family', felt a stupid, crushing disappointment.

Why? She had no time for a relationship. It was the last thing on her agenda. All she wanted in him was a reliable, trustworthy colleague.

So why did it matter so very, very much that he had a wife and family waiting for him at home?

The house was quiet. At the end of the hall he could hear the low murmur of the television from his parents' sitting room, and from above the subdued but still faintly audible beat of his daughter's little music system drifted down the stairs.

He'd threatened to take it away if she didn't moderate the volume. Apparently she was taking him seriously—either that or his parents had had words with her as well.

Otherwise, the house was peaceful and without obvious signs of bloodletting.

Heaving a sigh of relief, he went into the kitchen, pulled open the fridge door and studied the contents.

'I left you some supper. It's in the microwave.'

He straightened and turned towards his mother. She looked OK. No signs of a struggle, not a hair out of place, her face its usual calm, serene window on her untroubled soul.

He envied her that. Not the appearance. The untroubled soul. That he would give his eye teeth for, and probably a great deal more.

He kissed her cheek. 'You're a star. Everything OK?' he asked.

'Fine. Catherine's listening to music and reading, and Andrew's gone to sleep. The twins have been asleep for hours, I think the walk this afternoon exhausted them. How was work? Your new colleagues?'

He thought of Felicity, and something hot and dangerous and slightly terrifying came to life again inside him. 'Good,' he said, looking away from his mother's all too perceptive eyes and busying himself washing his hands at the sink. 'I think I'm going to enjoy working there. Very slick operation.'

And a nursing sister with a razor wit, enormous compassion and a body to die for—a woman that in his current circumstances he hadn't a prayer of doing justice to, even if he might be unbearably tempted, he thought with an inward groan.

'Oh, I am glad,' his mother said placidly, and he dragged his attention back to her. 'Chicken casserole, darling, or do you want to sit down for a minute first?'

His stomach rumbled, and he grinned, putting his need and frustration on one side and concentrating on the woman who at this moment was holding his world together. 'Mum, I love you. I'm starving. Bring it on.'

She laughed and pushed him into a chair, tapped the buttons on the front of the microwave and handed him a glass of wine. 'So it's going to be a success?'

'It's going to be great. All I need to do is find us a house and get some appropriate child care in place so we can get out of your hair and leave you in peace.'

Her face fell a little. 'You don't need to do that. You know I love having you all here, and so does your father. And the children need a woman's influence, especially Catherine. She's just at that age.'

'Tell me about it,' he groaned. 'Anyway, we wouldn't go far, and I don't suppose there's the slightest danger that we won't need you, whatever arrangements I make, so don't run away with the idea that you get your lives back entirely!' He was teasing, but there was an underlying element of truth in his words, and his dependence on his parents and their goodwill worried him. If only Jane—

'I don't want my life back. Your father and I were bored to tears sitting around looking at each other. Retirement doesn't suit us.'

'It should. You've earned it. I thought your business would be the death of you.'

She laughed. 'The death and the life. It's so strange without it—the days just hang, empty. The children are just the distraction we need.'

'But we're bursting at the seams here. Don't get me wrong, Mum, I'm hugely grateful, but welcome though it is as a temporary fix, your house just isn't big enough for us all long term. We'd end up killing each other.'

'So get a bigger one,' she said after a heartbeat, 'and we'll divide it up and live in it together. It'd be fun.'

He stared at her, stunned that she should come up with such a radical idea. Such a radical idea, and such a brilliant one. For him, at least, the prospect of having someone he could trust utterly with his children's safety and well-being was hugely appealing. And the loss of privacy didn't worry him in the slightest. There was no way he intended to get involved with a woman again in this lifetime.

Unbidden, an image of Felicity popped into his mind and nearly took his breath away.

Ridiculous. He didn't have time for a woman. Anyway, she was a colleague.

Probably married or otherwise taken, if there was a red-blooded man in Suffolk.

Although she hadn't had a ring on...

'I'll think about it.'

The microwave beeped, and spared him any further discussion for the time being, but later, after he'd run up and kissed Catherine good-night and checked on the other three, his mother brought up the subject again.

'About this house thing,' she said, in that considered tone that told him she'd thought it all out. 'Your father and I don't need a house this big any more, but it isn't big enough for all of us, as you so rightly pointed out. You need lots of upstairs space, and with your father's knee we're beginning to think we should be looking for somewhere without stairs.'

'So how does a bigger house work? It's just even more of a problem.'

'Not if you had all the upstairs and most of the downstairs, then we could have a couple of rooms downstairs so we'd all have our own space, but we'd be there for you when you needed us.'

They seemed keen, he thought, listening to their reasoning, as if they'd talked it through together at length. He needed time to think about it himself, though, and just at the moment time was in short supply.

And so were houses that big in his price bracket.

'I can't afford it,' he told them frankly.

'But *we* can—all of us, if we pooled our funds. We've got the money from the sale of the business—'

'That's your pension!' he protested, but his father shook his head.

'No. We have a pension in addition that's more than enough. We've been debating what to do with the money. Property's a sound investment—'

'Not always.'

'Long term it is.'

He gave up arguing, because he'd been casting around for a solution and this was far closer than anything he'd come up with yet.

'I tell you what,' he suggested. 'Why don't you canvass the agents and see what they can come up with? I'm going to be up to my eyes for the next week or two, settling into my new job and sorting out the kids' teething troubles with their new schools, but if you find something I'll happily look at it. I hate to pass the buck for the donkey work, but it could be a solution that suits all of us, if you really mean it.'

'Of course we do. Consider it done,' his father said, his eyes lighting up at the prospect of something to get his teeth into. 'Eileen and I'll get onto it in the morning.'

'And in the meantime you're not to worry. We're more than happy to have you all here for as long as it takes,' his mother said with conviction. 'Now, I don't know about you, but I'm going to make a drink and go up to bed. David?'

'I'll join you. I'll just put Amber out. Where is she?'

'Where do you think?' Tom said with a wry grin. 'Not that I approve of dogs on beds, but Andrew looked so comfortable with his arm round her I didn't have the heart.'

'I don't suppose it will do him any more harm than it did you. Do you remember when Bonzo used to sleep on your bed?'

He smiled. 'Oh, yes. I always knew when he had fleas.'

His mother chuckled. 'Right, I'm off—and you need an early night too, Tom. And don't worry. It'll be all right. We'll be here for you.'

And Tom, feeling the weight of some of his responsibility lift from his shoulders at her words, gave her a grateful hug, squeezed his father's shoulder on the way past and went to the little room that was his temporary home.

As a study it was fine. As a spare bedroom it left something to be desired, but it was better than sharing with Andrew, and after he'd washed and changed and settled down on the sofa bed, he lay staring up at the ceiling in the faint light that filtered through under the door and thought about his new job.

He was looking forward to it, he realised. Sure, it would be a challenge to settle into a new hospital, but today had been a brilliant way to get stuck in and get to know everyone.

And there she was again, right at the fore-front of his mind—the woman whose body had felt so right jammed up against his, whose every thought mirrored his own, and whose scent, even now, two hours later, was still filling his nostrils and tormenting the hell out of him.

She'd said something on the lines of 'See you tomorrow' as he'd been leaving, which implied she'd be on duty again.

Which meant he'd see her again in just a few hours.

No. He wouldn't think about her. He couldn't afford to get distracted. He had to keep his priorities right, and a woman was way, way down the list.

Even that woman. Perhaps *especially* that woman.

'Felicity.'

Without thinking, he said her name out loud, tasting it, rolling it around his tongue, and then he shut his mouth and gave a deep, growling sigh, turning onto his side and shutting his eyes firmly.

She was still there. He bashed the pillow into shape, rammed it back under his head and forced himself to count sheep.

Lots of them.

It was going to be a long, long night.

CHAPTER TWO

FLISS glanced at her watch and sighed. She really could have done without working late tonight, even if she had spent the last part of her shift with the most fascinating man she'd met in years.

A lot of good it would do her. Married, with children—the last thing she needed complicating her life. She had enough complications as it was—starting with this house.

It was already nine-thirty, and she had to be up for seven-thirty to let the builders in and programme them for the day. She was exhausted, and starting work on the house now was the last thing she wanted to do.

She would have done it yesterday, but she'd been ill, and with the plasterer coming in at seven-thirty tomorrow she didn't have a choice. The job was already running behind schedule, and if she didn't want to go hopelessly over budget, she had to get the units out of the kitchen, the remains of the old wallpaper stripped and the room cleared for Bill to start work first thing.

And that meant, of course, that she wouldn't have a kitchen for the next week or two. Great. She disconnected the sink, dragged the old unit out into the garden and went back for the cooker.

The guy who ran the Chinese round the corner would be pleased. She'd be eating take-aways for the foreseeable future, and heaven help her waistline.

Next job, before it was too late at night to make a noise, she used a hammer and bolster to whack the tiles off the walls, then shovelled the debris out and opened the window to let the dust out. There was something choking about lime plaster, she thought. Something choking about old houses and their dust gen-erally, perhaps. She must be mad.

The wiring had already been replaced, but she stripped out the old sockets from the room, all the time wondering why she did this when she had a perfectly respectable job.

She must be mad. Totally crazy. Only a complete lunatic would take on property developing on top of working full time in a demanding profession and running about after her widowed mother. Most women in their late twenties were nicely tucked up in their immaculate homes with their husband and children, not smashing plaster off walls and wrestling with stubborn old wiring.

She wriggled the last wire free, tugged it out of the socket and ripped it off the wall, then set about stripping off the remains of the wallpaper. Finally, just before twelve, she scraped away the last strip and stood back.

Done. Just a few more days and the units could go in, the new tiles on the walls and she'd be finished.

At midnight, after a full and very busy day hard on the heels of the department's stomach bug, the prospect of that last hurdle somehow seemed altogether too much, but at least it would keep her mind off Tom. She'd be too tired to see straight, never mind fantasise!

She needed a drink to settle the dust in her throat, but she couldn't find the glasses. Instead she pulled a can of beer out of the fridge, ran a hot bath and crawled into it, soaking away the stresses of the day and sipping the icy liquid while her mind, clearly not tired enough yet, drifted back to her new colleague.

Tom.

Even thinking his name made her skin come out in goose-bumps. Or perhaps it was the ice-cold beer. Whatever, working with him was going to be interesting.

Except, of course, that he was married with kids and responsibilities and commitments, she reminded herself firmly, and that put him severely off-limits. And anyway, she didn't need any more commitments herself. Fliss knew all about commitments. She had enough to sink a battleship, and the last thing she needed was to get entangled with a married man. Been there, done that. Never again.

She drained the can, balanced it on the edge of the bath and slid under the surface of the warm, welcoming water.

'Good weekend?'

Angie, the senior nursing sister in charge of A and E and Fliss's immediate boss, paused with her pen hovering over the whiteboard and smiled at Fliss over her shoulder. 'Lovely. I was in the garden for most of it—I'd forgotten how fast the weeds grow in spring. How about you? All better now?'

Fliss nodded. 'Yes, thanks, I'm fine now. Good job I am. Yesterday was hell.'

'I gather. I hear you met the new man.'

'I did. He popped in at the end of the afternoon, more fool him, and got dragged into the fray.'

'Mmm. Nick was very impressed—thought he was excellent.'

Fliss remembered his hands, sure and confident, working quickly and methodically and without error on patient after patient. She tried not to think about how they'd felt in her dream…

'Yes, he is, thank God. At least we won't have to babysit him while he settles in. Five hours in Resus was a bit of a crash course but I think he'll do!'

'You're too kind.'

She turned round, a smile on her lips and her heart already leaping into her throat. She struggled for casual and probably failed. 'Well, hello again. Did your family forgive you?'

He gave a low, wry laugh. 'They're used to me. It's hardly the first time. The youngsters were asleep—only Catherine was still awake by the time I got home.'

So his wife was called Catherine. Suddenly she hated the name. 'We'll have to make sure you leave on time tonight,' she said lightly, with what she hoped was a nice, neutral smile.

His chuckle sent shivers up and down her spine. 'You can try,' he said softly, 'but I don't fancy your chances if there's anything major going on. I'm not good at walking away from commitment.'

Although you looked to me last night as if you could quite easily step off the path for a while, if not walk away, she thought, reminding herself firmly that he was married and she didn't do relationships with married men. Ever. Under any circumstances.

In fact, it was so long since she'd had a relationship with anyone at all she wondered if she'd even remember how.

'So, what's going on today?' she asked both her colleagues. 'Anything big happened?'

'No, they're saving that for my knocking-off time,' Tom said good-naturedly. 'It's been nice and steady so far.'

'Three MIs,' Angie chipped in, 'a young man with a nasty headache that turned out to be a big bleed, lots of cuts and bruises and silly accidents, a couple of burns…'

'The usual, then.'

'Absolutely. There's a girl just finished in X-Ray who needs a back-slab on her wrist, Fliss, and there are a couple of cuts which need stitching when you've done that.'

'And I,' Tom said with a grin, 'am going to get some lunch before I fall off my perch. I'll see you all in a bit. Page me if anything exciting happens.'

'Be sure of it,' Fliss said, returning his smile, and then scooping up the notes she went off to put a cast on the young girl with the fractured radius. Her mother was with her, fretting and stressing about her daughter's tennis career, and Fliss struggled to reassure them both that it was a simple undisplaced fracture and should heal perfectly well given time.

'How much time?'

Fliss shrugged thoughtfully. 'I don't know. A couple of months? She won't be doing Junior Wimbledon this year, that's for sure, but there shouldn't be anything to stop her in the future.'

'But it's the start of the lawn tennis season! The timing couldn't be worse!'

Fliss smoothed the slab that cradled the underneath of Stephanie's damaged arm, checking the positioning of the limb. 'It's just one of those things. At least it wasn't a bad break.'

'It feels bad enough,' the girl said, her voice choked, and Fliss tutted gently and bandaged the back-slab carefully, allowing room for the limb to swell.

'It'll ease off soon when the painkillers kick in. It will ache, though, for a week or so, and you'll have to keep it up in a sling and come back tomorrow to the fracture clinic to have it checked. Then you'll have a proper cast on it once the swelling's settled down, and that will stay on about six weeks until they're happy the bone's healed. It may be quicker, it may not, but you've got youth on your side, and you need to keep your fingers moving once the pain's eased off a bit.'

'If it ever does,' Stephanie said unhappily.

'It will,' she said, wondering why the girl's mother didn't just hug her instead of fretting about her sporting career. After all, surely the girl was more important than her wretched tennis?

'I just knew something like this would happen,' Mrs Wright was saying. 'It was going too well. I just knew something would go wrong—you shouldn't have been climbing that wall.'

'Mum, it was a gym lesson! I didn't have a choice! And anyway, I like gym.'

'You like tennis, and now you can't play for weeks, and you'll lose your place on the county squad, and—'

'I really think this could keep until Stephanie's feeling a little better,' Fliss said firmly. 'For now, she needs your love and a little sympathy. Why don't you take her home and give her something light to eat, and tuck her up in bed?'

Mrs Wright shot her a quelling look, but Fliss shot it right back at her and after a moment the woman had the grace to colour and look away.

'You're right. Of course you are. I'm sorry, darling, I don't know what I was thinking about. Come on, let's take you home.'

'Don't forget to make an appointment for the fracture clinic tomorrow morning,' Fliss reminded them as they left, then cleared up and wiped down the table before leaving the plaster room for the next patient.

Two lots of stitching later, she emerged from the cubicles and found Tom in the staff-room with Nick Baker and Matt Jordan, laughing uproariously at a story Nick was telling about his little baby.

'Three of you here? Whoever did the rota must know something I don't,' she said lightly, and Nick chuckled and headed for the door.

'I'm out of here. I only popped in to pick up my mobile. I left it here yesterday, but I've seen quite enough of these four walls in the last forty-eight hours. I'll see you all on Wednesday morning.'

'And I've got some results to chase on a query MI, so I'm off, too.'

Matt walked out, leaving them alone. Fliss looked at the empty doorway and sniffed pointedly. 'Do I smell?'

Tom chuckled. 'Well, I didn't want to say anything...'

She threw a paper towel at him and picked up a mug, filling it with cold water from the tap and downing it in one. 'So, did you get your lunch without interruption?' she asked him, and he nodded.

'Amazingly. I tell you, all hell will break loose at about four. It always does—and yesterday was living proof.'

'Murphy's law?'

'Someone's,' he said with a chuckle. 'So, were you in trouble for being late last night?' he asked, propping his lean hips on the table beside her and studying her with open and blatant curiosity.

Her heart thumped and started to flail. 'Why should I be in trouble?'

He shrugged, a lazy smile playing around his lips. 'Just fishing.'

He's married, she reminded herself. 'Sorry. Nothing to catch. I live a solitary and blameless existence.'

He straightened and stared down into her eyes. 'What a tragic waste,' he said softly, and then headed for the door, leaving her alone with her jiggling heart and oxygen starvation.

*   *   *

Tom was right—not that it brought him any satisfaction. Four o'clock on the button they had a stream of ambulances bringing in GP admissions and a welter of accidents—the last of which, just as he was about to leave at six-thirty, was a young woman who had been knocked down by a car while crossing the road with her baby in a buggy.

Miraculously the tiny and very new baby seemed unharmed, but the young woman was critical, and everyone else was up to their eyes. What could he do?

What he always did, he realised, because to walk away was to consign her to certain death. He tugged on an apron and gloves and moved swiftly to her head, focussing absolutely on the patient and the paramedic who was frantically bagging her to maintain her respiration.

'We need to intubate,' he snapped, but Fliss put the laryngoscope in his hand before he'd finished the words, and the cuffed tube was at the ready. Within seconds it was in and the young woman's airway was secure. Fliss took over that end while he checked the heart monitor.

Well, she had an output, but that was all he could say for it. Thready, weak, irregular—her heartbeat was a mess, and he did a quick neurological screen and checked her level of consciousness.

'GCS is three,' he told them all. 'That's lousy. Her right pupil's fixed and dilated, the other one is pinpoint. We're looking at a major head injury here. She needs a scan, fast.'

But then she arrested, just as a young woman burst into the room and stood transfixed, her hands pressed to her mouth, her eyes like saucers.

'Jodie?' she whispered. 'Dear God, tell me she'll be all right! She was just there, next to me—'

'Someone take her to the relatives' room,' Tom said quietly. 'Charging—stand back!' He put the paddles of the defibrillator on her chest and shocked her, watching the monitor as she arched and flopped.

'Asystole,' Fliss said unnecessarily.

'Oh, God. Is my sister dead?'

'Not yet,' he said grimly. 'Relatives' room, please.'

But then he heard her deep breath, the steadying quality of it, the resolve in her voice. 'Let me stay. She would want me here. I should be here with her when she dies.'

And because the young woman was calm now, and because he agreed with her on so many levels, Tom let her stay and watch their fruitless attempts to save her sister's life.

And when those attempts failed again and again, and he straightened up and scanned their eyes, he saw the answer he'd been waiting for. 'I'm calling it,' he said quietly. 'Time of death seven forty-two. I'm sorry. Thank you, everyone.'

Stripping off his gloves and apron, he walked over to the young woman who was sagging against the wall, her fist rammed into her mouth, and laid his hand gently on her shoulder.

'I'm really, really sorry. There was nothing we could do, but if it's any comfort she didn't suffer.'

She nodded, the realisation stark in her eyes, and then she looked around her, the panic rising again. 'The baby—what happened to the baby? Oh, no—tell me she's all right!'

'The baby's fine,' Felicity said, appearing at his side. 'She's being taken care of. Come on, let's go and get you a cup of tea and you can come back and see your sister in a few minutes. Let's go and see if we can find the baby.'

And she put a comforting and supportive arm around her shoulder and led her away, while Tom went and filled in the requisite paperwork and told himself he hadn't been to blame.

He found the young woman with Felicity and two babies in the relatives' room a few minutes later. She was crying, silent tears streaming down her face as she breastfed one of the babies, and he frowned at it in confusion. He'd been sure the dead girl's baby was the newborn, and yet...

Felicity smiled at him, the other baby cradled asleep on her lap. 'Kate's just feeding her niece. They'd tried giving her a bottle but she wouldn't take it.'

'I've done it before. Jodie wanted to feed her, but she couldn't always manage. I've been doing it to top her up between feeds ever since they came home from hospital last week.'

She stroked the baby's soft, downy cheek and Tom felt a lump in his throat at the sight of this young woman so unquestioningly feeding her dead sister's baby, practicality taking over in the face of such overwhelming tragedy. 'She's so perfect,' Kate was saying. 'Jodie adored her, but she didn't really know how to look after her—she was head injured and she had learning difficulties. She got pregnant when she was raped at the day centre, by one of the lads she'd been at school with. He didn't really understand the significance of his actions, and nor did Jodie, but she understood what pregnant was because I was pregnant at the time, and she thought it was wonderful. We were the same for once...'

Her voice cracked. 'Could you phone my mum? She'll be wondering where we are, and I'm going to have to tell her about Jodie.'

'She's been called,' Tom said gently. 'I'll talk to her when she arrives. You just feed the baby and make sure she's all right. She's been thoroughly checked over and she's fine. She just needs love.'

'She'll get that,' the girl said, her voice fierce with promise, and Tom walked out fast before he made a fool of himself. Half an hour later, after he'd spoken to the girls' mother and answered all their questions, and only three hours after he should have left, he had a call from Catherine.

'Dad, there's water pouring out from under the kitchen sink all over the floor and Grannie and Grandpa are out and where *are* you?'

'Water?' he said, visions of a burst rising main filling him with panic. 'How much water?'

'Loads. It's *gushing* out of the bottom of the cupboard.'

Gushing. Hell. He stabbed a hand through his hair. 'OK, I'm coming home now. Put some towels down—'

'Towels?' she shrieked. 'Daddy, it's *ankle* deep!'

He swore, softly but with great feeling. 'OK. Move anything that's likely to get wet, and I'll be home in ten minutes. I'll try and get a plumber. Where are your grandparents?'

'Your parents,' she said pointedly, 'are out at a bridge evening. You knew that. They said you'd be home but I knew you wouldn't.' Her voice was at once accusing and victorious, and he sighed and rolled his head on his shoulders.

'OK. I'm coming now. Don't panic.'

He put the phone down and looked around at his colleagues. 'Anyone know where I can get a plumber at this time of night?'

They laughed, every single one of them, but then someone—Sophie?—pointed behind him.

'Try her.'

He turned, to find Felicity watching him warily. 'Try me for what?'

'I need a plumber. Water leaking out under the kitchen sink. Correction—gushing, according to Catherine. Do you know where I can find anyone at this time of night?'

She gave a defeated chuckle. 'In a manner of speaking. Where do you live?'

'Just outside the ring road, about half a mile from the cemetery on Tuddingfield Road. Why? You have a choice of plumbers?'

They all laughed again, as if they were sharing some private joke.

'Not exactly,' she said drily. 'Follow me home. I have to pick up some tools and I'll be with you. See you tomorrow, folks.'

And with that she turned on her heel and walked towards the door, pausing to look back at him as he stood there rooted to the spot.

'Well, do you want this leak fixed or not?' she asked, and he blinked, shut his mouth and followed her.

Fixing Tom's leak was the last thing Fliss wanted to do—especially if it meant she had to meet the hysterical Catherine—but she could hardly walk away from a colleague. And anyway, she was curious, dammit.

She churned the engine of her car until it finally caught, then drove home, keeping sight of him in her rear-view mirror. Not that she had a chance of losing him. His Mercedes was almost riveted to her bumper. Talk about tail-gating. Poor man must be desperate not to lose her!

She pulled up at the kerb outside her house, ran in with the engine still idling, grabbed her plumbing toolbox and ran back out again, then waved him ahead. He shot off down the road, and even knowing the roads as she did, she had trouble keeping up with him. Not that he was breaking the speed limit, but he didn't waste any time getting up to it after every junction, and her car was running like a pig. Still, he did seem to think it was an emergency.

Gushing, Catherine had said. Hmm. Could be fun. And she hadn't stopped to change, but there were some overalls in her boot, probably. That would have to do.

He turned into the drive of a large, neat post-war detached house, cut the engine and jumped out. She was three seconds behind him, and he had the door open and grabbed her toolbox before she could draw breath.

'Catherine?' he yelled, and a tall, slender girl of about thirteen or fourteen appeared in the hall, her eyes rolling.

'*Finally!*' she said, in the way only a teenager could manage, and Fliss suppressed a grin. Why did they always talk in italics?

'Catherine, I'm sorry,' he said, and Fliss blinked. Catherine? This was Catherine? So Catherine was not his wife, then, but his daughter, by the look of it.

Interesting.

She followed them into the kitchen, and suppressed a smile. OK, the floor was certainly wet, but it was hardly ankle deep, and the gush under the sink unit door was more of a dribble. She could hear the problem, though, and taking a deep breath she ducked her head inside, dragged out the contents of the cupboard and turned off the stopcock. The fine, drenching spray fizzled to a halt, and she wiped her face on the back of her arm and stood up, smiling ruefully at Tom.

'OK, I've stopped it,' she said. 'I can see

where it is. I'll get my overalls from the car and see if I can tighten the joint up, but it might be split just below it so I might have to join in a new section of pipe.'

'Right,' he said, looking blank but relieved that the water had stopped flowing, and she suppressed another smile and went out to fetch her overalls.

She was drenched already, of course, so the overalls were more to keep her clean than dry, but she didn't have another clean uniform at home and she didn't have the washing machine at the moment, so keeping clean was rather a priority. Wet she could cope with.

She went back inside and found Tom mopping the floor with towels and wringing them out in the sink, while Catherine half-heartedly poked the mop about and spread the water further.

She left them to it, taking a towel off Tom to mop out the bottom shelf before lying on it and staring up at the problem.

Hmm. A split, probably caused by knocking

the pipe. She found all the things she'd need for a repair and went back under the sink to deal with it.

How the *hell* could a woman with sopping wet hair and dressed in grubby, paint-splattered overalls possibly look so sexy? She was lying half in, half out of the sink cupboard, one leg straight, the other bent, pulling the overalls taut over that firm, delectable bottom as she arched up to get a better grip, and all he wanted to do was lie down there on the wet floor next to her and kiss her senseless.

For starters.

He twisted the towel so viciously over the sink that he heard the fibres give. Tough. It was the only way to work out his frustration— or at least the only way that was acceptable. To drag her out from under the sink and make love to her on the wet floor in front of his daughter really, *really* didn't qualify.

She struggled out from under the sink, pushing the hair out of her eyes with the back of her hand and smiling up at him victoriously.

'All done,' she said. 'I've turned the stop-cock back on—can you put the cold tap on and I'll make sure it's OK?'

He would have done anything for her at that moment. Turning the tap on was nothing. It seemed to satisfy her, though, because she gave him another of those sparkling smiles and stood up, tapping him on the nose with a damp, grubby finger.

'Smile. You're scowling. You'll get lines.'

'I've got lines,' he growled, and she laughed softly in his face.

'So you have. They suit you.'

Hell's teeth, she was flirting!

The blood was immediately diverted from his brain, and he dragged his eyes away from hers and mopped the floor as if his life depended on it.

She was packing up her tools beside him, crouched shoulder to shoulder on the floor, and he realised he hadn't thanked her. Hadn't said a word about anything sensible or relevant.

'Felicity, thank you,' he said, and as he opened his mouth to say more she raised a brow.

'Don't insult me, now,' she warned, and he gave her a wry grin.

'I wouldn't dream of it,' he said innocently, and her smile widened.

'Very sensible. Right, I need to go home and get out of these wet things.'

Now, why did she have to say that? The images it conjured up were enough to blow his mind, and he dragged in a nice, deep breath and stood up, hoping his body wouldn't embarrass him too much. The soggy towel dangling in front of him made an effective disguise, but then Catherine snatched it from him to wipe the floor and he grabbed Felicity's toolbox from her instead. By the time he handed it back to her outside they'd be in the dark and he might have had time to get his body under control.

'Right, I'm off.'

'Tom?'

His parents appeared in the doorway, took one look at the wet floor and Felicity in her overalls and were speechless.

He filled them in hastily, and his father immediately reached for his wallet.

Felicity shook her head. 'I don't charge friends,' she said firmly, and his face creased in puzzlement.

'Felicity is a nurse. She also happens to have plumbing skills, for some unknown reason,' Tom explained. 'Don't worry, Dad, it's taken care of,' he added, and ushered her out of the door before his mother, ever perceptive, realised just how much he appreciated his new colleague.

They followed, of course, showering Felicity with thanks and are you sures and how kinds, and she took her toolbox away from him before he was really ready to relinquish it, stowed it in the footwell and got behind the wheel.

And then her car wouldn't start. She churned and churned the engine, and then finally it caught, but it sounded like a bucket of bolts and he didn't fancy its chances of making it back to her place.

He opened her door. 'That sounds dreadful.'

'It *is* dreadful. It's desperately overdue for a service, but I just haven't got round to dropping it in, and I nearly ran out of petrol the other day. I expect that was the kiss of death—it's probably dirt in the fuel line. If it dies on me tonight, I'll scream.'

'Tom, you can't let her go home like that,' his mother said, ever practical. 'She might not make it. You'll have to follow her.'

'Or leave the car here and we'll get it serviced,' his father volunteered. 'The least we can do under the circumstances.'

'It's not necessary—'

'I'll follow you,' Tom said firmly, overriding her protests, and getting into his car, he reversed out onto the road, waited for her to turn round and pull out, and followed her back to her house.

Except she didn't stop at her house, she went on, turned into the next street and pulled up outside a garage. She put something—the key?—through the letterbox, ran back to him with her toolbox clanking against her legs and got in.

'I didn't think I was going to make it. I don't suppose you could give me a lift back to mine?'

'No, I'm going to make you walk,' he said drily, and, turning round, he drove back to her house and pulled up outside.

'Thanks.'

'No. Thank *you*. We would have been in deep do-do without your help tonight.'

She grinned. 'Nah. You would have opened the cupboard, turned off the stopcock and called a plumber in the morning.'

'If you say so. I'm still grateful. If you won't let me insult you, will you let me take you out to dinner?'

She laughed. 'In which spare minute, between us? Nice idea, though. In fact, have you eaten? There's a Chinese round the corner and I don't have a kitchen at the moment, but we could grab a quick set meal for two and a bottle of wine from the off-licence…'

'I'm driving,' he reminded her, but she just grinned impishly.

'So you are. You can have one glass—it just leaves all the more for me.'

He was tempted. He was ludicrously tempted.

She got out of the car, and without making a conscious decision he followed her.

'I need to get out of these wet things first,' she said over her shoulder as she went in, and he trailed her down the hall and into the room at the back.

It was a simple little Victorian terraced house, but she'd obviously been working hard on it and it showed. The walls were freshly painted, their feet echoed on the bare boards, and she waved a hand through a doorway at a gutted room with fresh plaster drying out on the walls and wires poking out all over it, presumably waiting for the sockets.

'The kitchen,' she said, dumping her toolbox on the floor and struggling out of the overalls. 'Or it will be. You see my problem with cooking at the moment!'

'And you're living here?'

'Where else? I don't have much choice.'

He shook his head. 'I'm amazed. How long have you been doing it up?'

'Five weeks,' she said. 'Another two to go and I can put it on the market.'

He blinked. 'The market? You mean, sell it, after all this hard work?'

'Yes, sell it,' she echoed, her voice teasing. 'I'm a property developer. It's what I do.'

He laughed softly. 'Pardon me. I rather thought you were a nurse.'

'Oh, that, too. Well, that first, really. This is what I do in my spare time.'

He laughed again, this time in disbelief. 'Spare time? You have that much spare time?'

'I don't have a social life,' she said frankly. 'It's better than the telly, and it means that in two more moves, I won't have a mortgage. I wouldn't be able to do that on a nurse's salary for years, if ever. And I like it.'

But he was stopped on the fact that she didn't have a social life. She'd said it before, when he'd been fishing for personal information. Maybe she really meant it.

'So—no man in your life, then?' he asked, just to be sure, and she chuckled ruefully.

'Are you kidding? Who'd put up with this?'

'I would,' he said quietly, after a heartbeat, and her eyes widened. 'I'm divorced. I've got four kids who've been gutted by their mother's desertion. There's no way on God's green earth I'll ever remarry and put my kids or myself in a position where we can be hurt like that again, but I'm lonely. I don't have a social life either, and I don't have time for one. I don't have time for someone who expects me to be home at a set time and free at the weekends and available to host dinner parties. But I...'

'Have needs?' she said softly.

He swallowed hard. 'Oh, yes. I have needs. All sorts of needs. Not just physical, but...'

She smiled. 'Me, too.' And without another word, she reached up on tiptoe, slid her arms around his neck and touched her lips to his.

He thought his heart would stop. Then he thought it would burst out of his chest.

Then he stopped thinking at all, and lost himself in the feel of her firm, supple body so beautifully aligned with his, and her lips, warm and mobile and parting slightly in invitation.

How could he refuse?

CHAPTER THREE

SHE hadn't meant to do this. She'd really, really intended to ask him in just for a drink, or perhaps the Chinese take-away they'd discussed.

But not this. Not offering herself to him on a plate in place of the meal!

And yet, meeting his eyes as he'd outlined the bare bones of his disastrous marriage, laid down the rules, talked about his needs, she'd realised she couldn't turn him away, not when those needs so exactly matched her own.

And she didn't want to turn him away, she realised as his hands came up and cupped her face, holding her steady as he hungrily, almost desperately deepened the kiss. His body was hard against hers, demanding a response, and she was powerless to withhold it.

Dammit, she didn't want to withhold it— didn't want to withhold anything from this man whom she hardly knew and yet knew better than she knew herself.

But she was grubby from struggling about under the sink, and her clothes were cold and soggy, and it was hardly the way she wanted their first time to be. Even with him addling her mind as he was with his clever kisses, she could see that clearly enough.

She eased away and looked up at him, gratified to see the raw hunger in his eyes, the masculine set of his jaw, his lips, full and firm and parted a fraction as his breath hissed through them roughly. Oh, yes, she thought. She could see him on a mountainside now, hewn out of granite, as raw as the elements.

She rested a hand on his chest and smiled.

Tom felt his heart lurch.

'I need a shower,' she said, her voice soft, husky, her eyes warm with promise. 'Come and join me.'

It would have taken a better man than him to walk away, and anyway, his legs didn't seem to be his own. He followed her up the stairs and into a beautifully fitted bathroom. He was dimly aware of the gleaming white suite, the sparkling chrome taps, the sharp, clean tiles.

But it was the luxurious shower cubicle that drew his attention. It filled one corner of the room, and already she was adjusting the tap, undoing buttons, stripping off her uniform.

She shot him a look over her shoulder. 'Well, are you coming?'

He made a rude noise, and she laughed softly, the sound muffled by the running water.

'Let me rephrase that. Are you joining me?'

'Both. Hopefully in the reverse order.'

Her hands reached up behind her back to undo her bra, and he dragged his eyes away. If he didn't want his fears to become reality, he was going to have to slow this down. Now, if only he could make his fingers work so he could undo his buttons…

'Changed your mind?'

'Not a chance.'

Finally free of his clothes, he stepped into the shower behind her, and she slid the door shut, turning into his arms. Her skin was cold, her nipples puckered and taut against his chest, and, desperate to taste her again, he anchored her head in his hands and plundered her lips beneath the pounding spray.

Her soft moan of need vibrated through his mouth, and he felt her hands slide down and round, cupping him. He dropped his head back against the tiles and tried to breathe, but he couldn't remember how. His hand caught hers, easing it away, his eyes pleading with her to go slow, but she didn't understand slow. She didn't want slow, obviously, because she bent one leg up and coiled it round his hip, and he was lost. He lifted her in his arms, turned her back against the tiles and drove into her in one swift, deep stroke.

She bit him, her teeth sinking into his shoulder, stifling the scream, and he lost the last fragile shred of control, his body driving, pulsing, spilling deep inside her.

He thought his legs would give way, but they didn't, by a miracle. He slumped against the wall, propping her up, his head dropping into the soft curve of her neck while his heart steadied and his breathing returned to normal, then he lifted his head and stared down into her wide, stunned eyes.

'Are you OK?' he said softly, and to his consternation her eyes filled with tears and she turned her head into his shoulder and wept silently.

He brushed the damp tendrils of hair away from her forehead. 'Felicity?'

She sniffed and lifted her head, scrubbing her nose on the back of her hand like a child, and he wiped the tears away with his thumbs and stared at her in consternation. 'Sweetheart, what's wrong? Did I hurt you?'

She gave a strangled little laugh, and then trailed her fingers over his jaw and gave him an unsteady smile. Her hand came to rest over his heart in a curiously protective gesture that brought a lump to his throat.

'Of course you didn't hurt me. It was fantastic. It was just—I don't know. I feel so silly, I never cry. I don't do this, either. I just don't. And I've never— I don't— I've never felt like that. So…connected. It just caught me by surprise.'

He stared at her for a moment, stunned that she'd described his feelings so precisely. For a few seconds he couldn't move, but then he drew her gently into his arms with a ragged sigh. 'I know,' he said, his voice choked.

He held her like that for a few more minutes until they'd both got their emotions under control, then eased her away and guided her back under the shower, wetting her hair and then lathering it, massaging her scalp with gentle, searching fingers, easing away the tension.

She rested her arms against the wall, her bottom propped against him, and he took the lather down over her body, soaping her with it, sliding his fingers over the full, firm mounds of her breasts, the slender line of her waist, the flat bowl of her abdomen, down over the nest of curls to cradle them gently.

She turned into his arms, her eyes calm now, serious, and taking a blob of shower gel she lathered him all over, returning the favour.

'It's a good job I've got a boiler that makes endless instant hot water,' she said pragmatically as she soaped him, and he chuckled, the laugh turning to a strangled sob as her fingers circled him.

He shackled her wrist and eased her hand away, determined this time to make it last.

'No. Not here. Not again. My legs won't take the strain. I take it you do have a bed?'

She laughed, a warm, soft sound that made his blood surge in his veins.

'Oh, yes,' she promised. 'I have a bed. It's a very comfortable bed.'

'Good, because that's more than can be said for your shower, endless hot water or not. Let's get rid of the soap, dry off a bit and take it slow.'

Her smile was as old as time.

'Slow sounds good.'

Looking at her there, with the soft glow of loving in her eyes and the sheen of water on her skin, he wondered if it was a vain hope...

She couldn't believe it. There they were, sitting cross-legged in the middle of the tumbled quilt, eating hot buttered toast and sipping tea, him looking ridiculously sexy in his jersey boxers with that soft, dark hair arrowing down his chest and disappearing enticingly under the waistband, and her in a baggy old T-shirt that had definitely seen better days and a pair of knickers to preserve her modesty, although it was probably too late for that. There was no tension between them, no morning-after regret or nonsense like that.

Amazing.

Not that it was morning yet. Not really—although it was after midnight, so technically it qualified.

He bit into the toast, his clean, even, white teeth sinking into the crisp surface and tearing it, and she nearly groaned aloud. How on earth could that turn her on?

Easy. It seemed that everything about him turned her on, in a way that nothing and no one ever had before.

He hitched the pillows up behind him and leant back against the wall, sighing content-edly. His eyes were tracking over her, and there was warmth and tenderness in them, and a slight smile played around his firm, sculpted lips.

'What?' she said, suddenly uncertain under his scrutiny. 'Have I got a crumb on my nose or something?'

The smile widened, and he shook his head. 'No. Nothing. I'm just enjoying looking at you.'

'Heaven knows why. I look a sight.'

'You look gorgeous.'

She laughed ruefully and shook her tousled, still-damp hair off her face. 'Yeah, right—and the man needs his eyes tested. I look a complete fright, and if I don't want to look just as bad tomorrow I must remember to rescue my uniform and press it. I haven't got another one clean and I'm on duty at seven tomorrow.'

'How are you getting there?'

She shrugged. 'I'll walk. It's not far. Takes about fifteen minutes. It might do me good.'

'I'd offer you a lift but I'll be embroiled in breakfast and packed lunches by then.'

It sounded homely and comforting, and she was suddenly vividly aware of just how lonely and isolating her life was. Not that she would change it. She had a plan, and she was sticking to it, come hell or high water—or the sexiest man she'd ever met in her life. Not that changing her life for him was an option anyway.

'Lucky you,' she teased, trying to keep her voice light. 'Think of me up to my eyes in other people's blood.'

He tipped his head on one side and studied her, his face serious now. 'Do you enjoy your job?'

'Which one?'

'The nursing.'

'Yes,' she replied honestly. 'I love it—well, mostly. I love it when we can drag people back from the brink. I'm not so keen when we lose them.'

'Like Jodie,' he said quietly, and she nodded.

'Like Jodie. Poor girl, she already had enough strikes against her. I wonder if the baby will be all right. At least she wasn't injured. Do you think Kate will look after her?'

'Probably. I had a chat with their mother,' he told her. 'It was the organ donation chat, really, but it brought up a lot of other issues. She said Jodie had been brain damaged as a toddler—she fell off the outside of the staircase into the hall and hit her head.'

'Oh, no. Kate said she'd been head-injured, I didn't know how. I wonder if the mum feels guilty for that.'

'I'm sure she does. I know I would.'

Fliss wondered what it would be like to have a child and feel such a sense of responsibility. Terrifying, she decided. 'What about the baby's father? Do you know anything about him?'

'Apparently he'd had a brain tumour in his early teens, and they operated to save his life and it left him with brain damage. Hell of a trade-off, but at least the baby won't have inherited any genetic hiccup from either of them. The family have got enough to cope with in terms of guilt and grief, without that to add to it.'

'Absolutely. I feel so sorry for them all.'

'Her mother was talking as if she'd been given a second chance with Jodie, in a way. I'm sure there's a lot of leftover guilt from Jodie's accident, and maybe she sees this as a chance to atone for that guilt—both by donating Jodie's organs, which she agreed to do, and by bringing up the baby.'

'I'm sure Kate will be involved, too,' Fliss said, remembering how unquestioningly she'd fed her sister's baby. 'She's on her own apart from her mother, and lives with her, but she's got her own baby to deal with. They'll probably share their upbringing. I suppose it'll be like having twins,' she added thoughtfully, and Tom gave a strangled laugh.

'Yes—and I wish her luck. It was twins that sounded the death knell of my marriage. It was bad enough that Jane got pregnant by accident for the second time—'

He broke off, staring at her in horror, and then rammed his hands through his hair and shook his head in disgust. 'And I've just done it again! I don't believe this. With my history I can't believe we just made love twice without taking any precautions. I must be insane. Talk about not learning from your own mistakes.'

'Don't worry,' she said quickly. 'It's OK, I'm on the Pill.' Not that she would have given it a moment's thought, either, so it was just as well she was. What an idiot!

Tom was looking relieved, but also a little puzzled. 'I thought there wasn't anyone in your life?' he said, and she wasn't sure, but she had a feeling there was a slightly territorial tone in his voice. She could set his mind at rest on that score as well.

She shook her head. 'There isn't. I had a relationship a couple of years ago—with a property developer, oddly enough. I kept bumping into him at open house viewings and auctions and things, and we drifted into an affair. It ended rather abruptly when his wife came into the same restaurant one lunchtime with a group of her friends.'

'Ah.'

'Indeed. I said rather more than that,' she told him, glossing over it lightly because she would really, *really* rather not rehash the whole sordid incident ever again. 'Anyway, the only good thing that came of it was I realised my cycle was much more regular and my periods much less troublesome while I was on the Pill, so I've stayed on it, so in a way he did me a favour.'

His laugh was a little strained. 'Talk about looking on the bright side.'

She shrugged. 'You have to. I try and find the good in every situation. If you don't, life can be a pretty rum old thing.'

'Tell me about it.' He glanced at his watch and sighed heavily. 'It's nearly one, and you have to be at work with your uniform pressed in six hours. I'd better get out of your hair.'

'So that's what's wrong with it,' she said with a grin, picking up a hank of the spiky, rumpled mess that she'd failed to comb after her shower. 'Or could it be that I was distracted?'

'I don't know what you mean.' He laughed and dropped a hot, searing kiss on her lips before climbing off the bed and padding through to the bathroom to look for his clothes.

She almost followed him, but common sense told her to let him go. He had a family to get back to, and she refused to let herself get clingy. She knew the rules. He'd told her quite clearly what he could offer her, and God knows she didn't have much to offer in return.

So she stayed there, curled up in the crumpled quilt amidst the toast crumbs, and moments later he was back, fully dressed and with her damp uniform dangling from his fingers.

'I'm really sorry you got soaked—and I still owe you dinner.'

She got off the bed and went over to him, going up on tiptoe and pressing a gentle, undemanding kiss on his lips. 'You owe me nothing. You've just given me the night of my life.'

'No regrets?'

'Never. It was the best.'

He smiled slowly. 'Me, too. You take care. I'll see you in the morning.'

He backed away, ran lightly down the stairs and she heard the front door click shut behind him, the sound loud in the empty hall.

She glanced down at the uniform in her hand, shrugged and stuck it on a hanger on the back of her door. She'd worry about it in the morning. For now, she had better things to do.

She crawled into bed, breathed deeply and smiled. His scent was on the sheets, male and uniquely his, and she snuggled the quilt up under her nose and fell asleep in seconds.

'She seems a nice girl.'

'Huh?'

'Felicity.'

Tom swallowed hard and busied himself with his toast. 'She is,' he said, wondering if his mother would think she was such a nice girl if she'd seen them in the shower last night.

'Your father says she's done a very neat job.'

'Good.'

'So—I take it she's single?'

'I believe so—and before you get any ideas, so am I, and I'm staying that way, so don't start. She's just a colleague.'

'If you say so, darling. Of course, you know best.' His mother's eyes widened innocently, but he wasn't fooled. He gulped down his coffee, crammed in the last mouthful of toast and went to hassle the children.

'We've got ages yet,' Andrew grumbled, hardly taking his eyes off the book that was his constant companion.

'He hasn't cleaned his teeth,' Catherine said smugly, emerging from the bathroom with eyelashes that looked just a touch too dark to be true.

'Hasn't he, indeed. Andrew, teeth. Catherine, get that make-up off, please. You know you aren't allowed to wear it.' Ignoring the denials and grumbling protests, he went into the twins' bedroom and found them fighting over a reading book.

'It's mine!'

'No, it's mine!'

'Actually it belongs to the school. Now give it to me before you rip it in half,' Tom said patiently, holding out his hand. Abby slapped the book into it with very little grace and flounced off, arms folded over her skinny little chest, chin stuck out and pouting for England.

He suppressed a smile and chivvied Michael who, having won the book argument, by his reckoning, was lounging back on his bed poking his tongue out at his sister and doing nothing to hasten his progress out of the door.

'Come on. We have to go. Get up, comb your hair and put your shoes on—and tuck your shirt in while you're at it.'

'Don't want to.'

'Tough. We all have to do things we don't want to do. Come on.'

He came, grumbling under his breath, and was joined on the landing by his older sister, sporting considerably less make-up but a pout even better than Abby's, and Andrew, teeth more or less cleaned and his nose back in his book. Abby was sitting on the stairs looking hard done by, and Tom resisted the urge to

grab the lot of them and bang their heads together.

Twenty minutes later they were delivered,
albeit reluctantly, to their respective schools,
and Tom was pulling up in the hospital staff
car park.

He looked for Fliss's car, but it was at the
garage, of course. He'd forgotten. He wondered if she'd managed to get in all right, and
then chastised himself for being stupid. Of
course she had. And anyway, it was hardly his
responsibility or any of his business.

But he found himself hurrying for the door,
his stride lengthening absurdly in his haste to
be inside and see her again. He forced himself
to slow down, to take deep breaths, to lecture
his body on appropriate and acceptable stan-
dards of behaviour, then the doors swished
open and she was there, as if his wishful thinking had conjured her up out of thin air.

He stopped in his tracks, his mouth kicking
up in an involuntary smile. 'Welcoming com-
mittee?' he said, and she laughed, but her eyes
were soft and held a gentle affection.

'Don't get too excited. I'm expecting an ambulance any second.'

'I'm heartbroken.' He ran his eyes over her critically, and grinned. 'You got the creases out, then.'

She glanced down at her uniform and gave a rueful smile. 'More or less. It won't stand close inspection, though, and my hair's still got knots in it.'

'I'll have to remember not to study you too closely,' he said, trying hard not to think about how she'd got the knots in her hair. 'So, what are you expecting in the ambulance?'

'A baby with what sounds like epiglottitis.'

He felt the smile slip and the professional kick in. 'Paediatrician standing by?'

'And anaesthetist. They're on their way to the department. I'm just providing a calming influence for the mother. We don't want to push the little one into a crisis.'

He nodded, waiting with her as the ambulance, right on cue, pulled carefully up to the doors and the mother emerged, cradling a gasping toddler and looking utterly panic-stricken.

'Mrs Keyes? Why don't you come with me,' Felicity said, her voice calm and quiet and re-assuring, and Tom took the handover infor-mation from the paramedics in the ambulance and followed her in. Within moments, Mrs Keyes and her baby were safely in the hands of the paediatric specialists, and he let out the breath he hadn't known he was holding and smiled at Felicity.

'Well done, you really held her together. It's so easy to precipitate a crisis with epiglottitis. The last one I saw was nearly fatal because the mother insisted on opening the child's mouth to show me and the throat just closed. By the time she'd finished having hysterics it was nearly too late.'

'But you came flying in on your white charger and saved the day,' she teased, and he chuckled.

'Of course,' he agreed, and their eyes locked and held. His body forgot the lecture he'd just given it and went into hyperdrive. 'Felicity, about last night...' he began, and her chin lifted in a touchingly defensive gesture.

'I know. It didn't mean anything. It's OK, I understand the rules.'

She turned away, but he caught her arm and turned her back. 'I wasn't going to say that at all. I was actually going to say thank you.'

'For the plumbing?'

'For all of it. The plumbing, and the rest.' His voice lowered. 'Most particularly the rest.'

Soft colour swept over her cheeks and her eyes warmed, but she didn't look away. 'It was a pleasure,' she murmured. 'Any time.'

'Don't tempt me,' he growled under his breath. 'I'm sure there's a linen cupboard or a storeroom somewhere in this hospital.'

Her laugh was wry and full of good-natured regret. 'I wish. Tom, I need to get on.'

'So do I. See you later.'

She nodded and turned away, absorbed within seconds into the relentless processing and treatment of patients. He watched her for a few seconds, then headed down the corridor, feeling more content than he had done for ages.

She was just what he needed—warm, affectionate, intelligent, mature—and sufficiently independent that she wouldn't make demands he hadn't a prayer of meeting.

Perfect.

Humming quietly under his breath, he went into the office shared by the consultants, dumped his coat and rolled up his sleeves, then went to join the throng.

How odd. Fliss had wondered what it would be like when they bumped into each other this morning, and it had been easy. No strain, no atmosphere—well, not until she'd jumped to conclusions about what he'd been going to say on the subject of last night, and then it had only been a micro-second before he'd put her straight.

And then tied her in knots again, so that her heart had flapped against her ribs and tried to choke her. She was going to have to learn to control her reaction to him better than this, or she was going to end up a patient herself! Oh, well, she'd just bury herself in work and maybe she wouldn't have to spend too much time with him today. That would give her a little space to get her emotions back under control.

In fact, the rest of the morning was so busy she didn't have time to think about him, but then as fate would have it she took her lunch-break at the same time as Tom, and ended up being talked into lunch in the canteen.

'Don't imagine this lets you off buying me dinner,' she teased, looking down at the congealed chicken curry and clumpy rice that had been the best of a bad lot so late in the day.

'As if I would be so cheapskate,' he said in mock reproach, and then blew it all with his next words. 'Actually, I've got a confession. I wanted to talk to you about houses.'

'Houses?' she repeated, feeling an odd sense of disappointment that he didn't just want to spend time with her for herself—but, then, why should he? She'd obviously have to keep reminding herself that as far as he was concerned, wonderful though it might have been last night, they were just scratching each other's itches.

Full stop.

Dammit.

'So,' she said, poking at her curry with a fork and wondering if she was really that hungry, 'what do you want to know?'

'Where to start, really. My parents and I are talking about buying a large house together and converting it into two separate but connected dwellings, to solve some of my childcare issues. The trouble is, it needs to be huge to fit us all in comfort, and the budget isn't bad but it's not as big as it'll probably need to be. Any ideas where we should start?'

She shrugged thoughtfully. 'The local paper has a property section on Thursday. That's as good a place as any, or you could try the internet. What are you looking for?'

He looked puzzled. 'Well—like I said, somewhere big.'

'But old or modern? Do you want land? How close to the hospital, and what about school catchment areas?'

He stared at her in frustration. 'Good grief. I don't know. A garden for the kids, some-where safe. School catchment isn't important, they're already enrolled in independent schools because I knew we'd be moving and I didn't want to risk disrupting them again. A period house, I suppose, for preference, but in good condition.' His mouth quirked into a wry smile. 'I'm not a DIY enthusiast, as you will have gathered from the plumbing incident.'

Fliss chuckled. 'You don't say. What about distance from the hospital?'

He shrugged. 'Ten minutes in the car?'

'OK. I'll think about it and keep my eyes open, but don't hold your breath. Talking of cars, I've had a call from the garage. Apparently I've got a blocked fuel line. I bet it's because I used a grotty old petrol can of my father's to top it up when I thought it was going to run out.'

'So will it cost a lot to sort out?'

She shrugged. 'I have no idea. Depends where the blockage is, I guess. All I know is I'll be another day or so without it, and at this moment in time, I really don't need that. I can't believe I was so stupid, but I didn't think. I know nothing about cars, and I don't treat mine with any respect at all. I think it's just having a well-earned flounce.'

He chuckled. 'Very likely. And I'm amazed you know nothing about cars. I thought you knew everything about everything,' he teased, and she dipped her finger into her glass and flicked water at him.

'You're rude.'

'And you're extraordinarily talented,' he said, abandoning his teasing tone in favour of a quiet sincerity that brought a lump to her throat. 'You've obviously got very sound practical skills, and I don't think I've ever worked with a nurse who was so totally focussed and intuitive. And on top of all that you're funny, and beautiful, and great company.'

So much for thinking he didn't want to spend time with her! She felt a soft wash of colour over her cheeks, and looked away, immeasurably touched by his words.

'You're such a sweet-talker—and anyway, you're pretty good with your hands yourself,' she replied, thinking of his skill with the patients, but his strangled laugh made her look up and she realised he'd misinterpreted her words.

'You're too kind,' he said. 'Should I be flattered?'

'Idiot! I meant medically,' she pointed out, struggling to keep a straight face, but he was still laughing, and she found herself joining him.

It was only later, after she'd walked back to the department with him and found herself listening all afternoon for the sound of his voice, that she realised how deeply entrenched she was and how important he was becoming to her. If she wasn't careful, her heart was going to be involved as well as her body and her mind, and that would be disastrous.

She didn't do love, and neither did he, and she'd do well to remember it.

CHAPTER FOUR

SHE got her car back on Wednesday night, quicker than expected, and on Thursday she bought the paper on her way into work, to see if the agent had advertised her little house as he'd said he might. It wasn't finished, of course, but there was only another weekend's work to do and it would be ready, and the sooner she could sell it, the sooner she could move on.

To her surprise it was advertised in the paper, and for more than they'd discussed. Fliss shrugged. Oh, well, if he was going to make a mistake, better that way than the other, and it looked like a good photo of the front. Kerb appeal, she thought, and smiled in satisfaction, then threw the paper to one side and hurried to the hospital.

When she arrived at ten to seven, the place was already humming, so she dropped her bag and jacket in her locker and went to join the fray. 'Want to do the handover now?' she asked the night sister, but Sue shook her head.

'It's chaos this morning.' She pointed towards the front of the building. 'Tackle that lot, could you, my love? We've got a three-hour waiting time already, and most people aren't even up yet. I'll hang on for a bit and do the handover when Angie gets here at nine.'

'Right, I'll get stuck in.'

She took the notes from the rack by the reception desk, and called the next patient on the list. An hour later she'd dealt with three cuts, a kettle scald and a trip over the cat on the front doorstep. She heard Tom arriving with Matt, heard the good-natured banter, and told herself that she'd get a heart condition if she didn't stop reacting to the man's voice like that.

Telling herself to be sensible and keep things in perspective, she went back out to Reception and called the next patient. The name was familiar to her, and she recognised the man instantly as he stood up and inched painfully towards her. He was wearing his white overalls, so he'd obviously had an accident at work, and judging by the way he was moving, he was very sore.

She went to meet him. 'What's up, Bill? Couldn't you stay away from me?' she teased, studying him carefully as he hobbled the first couple of steps.

His mouth twitched into a pained grin. 'I might say the same about you. What are you doing here?'

'My other job,' she said with a smile. 'Come on through, let's have a look at you. What hurts?'

'My ankle—well, the outside of my leg, really, I suppose, but it's all a bit of a blur, pain-wise.'

'OK, we'll get you in a wheelchair so you don't have to walk on it. Hang on.'

She helped him into a chair, propped his leg up on a pillow and wheeled him through to the cubicles. 'Right, I'll just take your shoe off and have a quick look, but I expect it'll need an X-ray. What happened?'

'Oh, I tripped over a bucket of plaster in my stilts.' His voice was full of disgust, but underneath it she could detect anxiety. Like many people in the building trade, he couldn't afford to take time off sick because he was self-employed, and Fliss would bet her lunch that he was already worrying about how long this would take to sort out. His next words confirmed it.

'Just don't find anything,' he said as she lifted his leg carefully and eased his overalls up to reveal his ankle. 'I don't mind a sprain, but I can't afford a fracture, not at this time of year. Things have been a bit lean over the winter and work's really piling in now.'

She tipped her head and smiled at him. 'Well, you've finished my plastering, anyway, so I'm all right. I'll forgive you.'

Bill laughed, as he was meant to, but removing his shoe and sock soon wiped the smile off his face.

'Sorry, I know it hurts, but it has to come off.'

'I know. Don't worry, love. It doesn't look bad enough to hurt that much,' he said, peering doubtfully at the side of his ankle. 'Maybe I just bruised it badly—probably hit it on something on the way down.'

'Mmm. There's definitely bruising there, but not much swelling and it doesn't look superficial. I think we need a picture of it. I'll get a doctor to look at you. He'll probably order X-rays.'

'Is that necessary, if it's just bruised? Only I've left my boy finishing the ceiling, and he's not really up to it yet. I ought to get back—'

'Yes, it is necessary,' she said firmly, but softened it with a smile. 'You aren't going anywhere until that's thoroughly checked out, Bill. I'll get a doctor. Won't be two ticks.'

She was even less time than that, because as she opened the curtain, Tom was there emerging from the neighbouring cubicle. He glanced across at her and raised an eyebrow.

'Want me?' he asked, and she felt her colour threaten to rise. She forced herself to ignore the twinkle in those wickedly expressive eyes.

'I've got an old friend of mine in here—Bill Neills. He's a plasterer. He's fallen over in his stilts and done his ankle.'

'Ouch. Any swelling?'

She shrugged. 'Not much. Bruising, though, starting to come out at the bottom of his fib. Looks like he's gone over on it and turned the foot in.'

He nodded and followed her back through the curtain, introducing himself to Bill and putting him at his ease. 'So you're a plasterer, are you? You've got my deepest admiration. I can't even put a cast on with any style, never mind plaster a ceiling. I don't know how you do it.'

'Well, I faint at the sight of blood, Doc, so we're quits, I guess.' He looked down at his leg, concern clouding his eyes. 'So, what about this, then? Can you strap it up and let me go? I really can't afford any time off. I was telling Fliss, I've left the lad to finish off, but he's only training.'

'Let's see, shall we?' Tom crouched down, using his eyes first to assess the injury before taking hold of Bill's foot in his hands and moving it carefully from side to side. His fingers probed gently but firmly at the injury, and Bill grunted with pain.

'I'm sorry, I know it hurts but it's necessary to know the range of movement. Can you push against my hand?' Another gasp, and Tom straightened and looked him in the eye.

'Right. It doesn't want to flex in towards the centre, you can't press down and I don't like the look of that bruising. I want a few X-rays of that from different angles, and we'll go from there, but my gut feeling is it's a fracture, Bill. I'm sorry. I know it's not what you want to hear, and I might be wrong, but I don't think so. Let's find out.'

He turned back to the desk, scribbled on an X-ray request form and handed it to Fliss. 'OK. I want a full set of plates on that. Can you give me a shout when they're done?'

'Sure. Thanks.'

Bill stared at his leg in consternation. 'So I did break the bloody thing, then.'

She gave him a rueful smile and knocked the brakes off the chair. 'Maybe. Let's not jump the gun. We'll get your X-rays first.'

'The doc thinks it's broken—and you do, too. I can see it in your eyes, Fliss. I may only be a plasterer but I'm not a fool.'

'Only a plasterer?' She snorted. 'I couldn't do your job in a hundred years. That's why I use you. You're a fine craftsman. Don't worry, we'll soon have you back on your feet.'

'Not before the boy's finished the ceiling.'

'The ceiling will be fine. Give your son credit, he's a good lad, and he couldn't have had a better trainer.'

She parked him outside X-Ray, passed his notes through to the radiographer and patted his shoulder reassuringly. She couldn't wait with him, there were too many other people waiting for her attention, but she kept an eye on the queue and retrieved him as soon as he was done.

'Well?' he asked, but she shook her head.

'Mr Whittaker has to look at the plates, Bill.'

'But you could tell me.'

She sighed and shook her head, smiling to soften her words. 'What would I know? I'm a property developer, not a doctor.'

'You see the flaws in my work soon enough,' Bill said drily, and she chuckled.

'Don't worry. He'll be in in a minute. I'll go and chivvy him up.'

She found Tom just finishing an examination, and handed him the envelope with the X-rays in it. 'Bill's plates,' she explained, and he snapped them onto a light box and frowned at them thoughtfully.

'Well, he's been lucky. There's a hairline crack—see it? Just there, on the fibula. He must have gone over sideways, but he's lucky it's such a minor injury, considering what he could have done coming off those stilts.'

Fliss laughed. 'I'll let you tell him how lucky he is. I don't think he'll agree.'

'Passing the buck?'

She smiled. 'Hardly mine to pass. I'm just a simple nurse,' she said innocently, and he snorted, whipped the plates off the light box and went in to Bill, leaving her chuckling in his wake.

'Right, Bill—d'you want the good news or the bad news?'

'I know the bad news,' the man said drily. 'What's the good news?'

'It's only a hairline crack, and if Felicity puts a lightweight cast on it, you'll only be off work for a few weeks—five at the most, I would say, but you'll probably need to avoid the stilts for a while until it's healed up completely.'

Bill grunted. 'And that's the good news?'

'I'm sorry. The way you fell, you could have ended up in Theatre, so, yes, it is the good news. I'll leave you in Felicity's capable hands.'

'Felicity, eh?' Bill said when they were alone again. 'Thought your name was Fliss.'

'I answer to anything that's not rude,' she told him, but when she thought about it, she realised Tom only ever called her Felicity. Most people called her Fliss, unless they were being formal for any reason, or were cross with her. She'd been called Felicity a lot in her childhood, she thought wryly—but somehow, when Tom said it, it sounded different.

Lyrical, somehow. Rather beautiful.

And she was in danger of losing her marbles.

'Right, Bill, let's get this leg in a cast and get you home to rest,' she said, wheeling him through to the plaster room and helping him up onto the couch.

'Oh, that feels better,' he said, when she'd wrapped his leg in wadding and was carefully winding the lightweight cast bandage around it to immobilise it. 'A bit safer. I hadn't realised it was so fragile.'

She smiled understandingly at him. 'People always say that. I'll put a heel into it so you can walk on it, but you need to give it a few days before you do that, so I'll only put the heel in if you promise me faithfully to keep off it at first,' she said, her voice stern, but Bill had known her a long time now and he just grinned.

'You know I can't promise that,' he told her.

Her hands stilled. 'Bill, you have to,' she said seriously. 'If you don't give this injury time to heal, it'll be a lot worse for you in the long run. So what's it to be—am I putting a heel in and you're using your common sense, or do I make it impossible for you to walk and you'll have to come back and have the cast changed in a week or so?'

He sighed, realising at last that she meant what she said, and raised his hands in submission. 'I'll be sensible. I can't afford to waste any more time than I have to.'

'Good. And that means you won't be back at work until the cast's off—or at least, only in a supervisory capacity. You'll have to let your son assume some responsibility.'

His eyes slid away, and she gave a resigned sigh and finished the cast. It was up to him. She'd warned him, Tom had warned him—if the man wanted to take risks, he was big enough and ugly enough to make up his own mind.

'Right, all done. Now get yourself fixed so you're ready for my next job.'

He laughed. 'Anything lined up?'

'Not yet. Heard of anything coming up?'

'Not really. Not in the sort of state you usually take them on.'

She thought of Tom's requirements. 'What about something bigger? A lot bigger.'

'Bigger? Well, funny you should say that, because the wife told me about one last night—not your usual sort of thing at all. Bloody great big place.'

She cocked her head on one side, her interest piqued. 'Really? Where is it?'

'I reckon you know it—the Red House, out at Tuddingfield, near your mother. The old dears have finally gone into a home, I hear, and it's coming up for auction. Should be right up your street if you could afford it—it's falling down, it's got no facilities to speak of and it needs a bit of your magic. Trouble is, it's about ten times the size of your usual project, and probably about ten times the price.'

She felt a familiar tingle in her veins, the tingle she always felt if a property was a real gem—and this one was. If Tom wanted space, the Red House would give it to him in spades—and she'd get to look inside it, something she'd been aching to do for years.

'So who's the agent?' she asked, the excitement starting to bubble inside her.

'Don't know, but the wife heard it from the postmistress in the village.'

Fliss laughed. 'Well, if anyone knows, it'll be June. I'll get my mother on it.'

'Are you serious? Do you want it?'

She shook her head. 'I don't, but I know a man who does—or might. Thanks for telling me. I'll pass it on.'

'Try and get me the plastering contract. I'd love to see that old place restored.'

She smiled thoughtfully. 'You and me both, Bill. And if I can get you the job, I promise you I will—if you promise to be sensible.'

He drew his hand across his chest. 'Cross my heart and hope to die,' he said, but she didn't believe him for a moment.

'Go on, down you get. I'll find someone to fix you up with some crutches, and then you can go home and put your leg above the level of your heart until tomorrow morning. You'll need to come back to the fracture clinic then just to make sure the cast isn't too tight and everything's looking all right, but if you have any problems with it, if it feels tight or your toes swell or get discoloured or feel tingly before tomorrow, you're to come back straight away. OK?'

He nodded, his face suddenly serious. 'I will. Thank you, Fliss. It's nice to know you're as good at this job as you are at the other. I might have known you would be.' He squeezed her hand in thanks, and looked away, suddenly awkward, the back of his neck ruddy with embarrassment.

'You're just trying to get round me so I won't call you back when the ceilings crack,' she teased, breaking the tension, and then she flicked the brakes off and pushed him out, gave some painkillers, then found the technician in charge of fitting people for crutches and left them to it.

Tom was in the staffroom, grabbing a quick coffee, and she grinned at him.

'Found a house yet?'

He snorted. 'In which spare minute? I had a look through the paper, but there was nothing in it for under a million that caught my eye.'

'Such unerring good taste,' she teased, and poured herself a coffee. 'I might have found you something. How does Tuddingfield sound?'

'Tuddingfield? Isn't that just out beyond my parents', about a couple of miles further out?'

She nodded. 'Bill told me about a place. It's wonderful—or it will be.'

'Will be?' he echoed warily.

Fliss hid a smile. 'Trust me. If I find out about it, do you want to view it?'

He shrugged. 'It won't hurt to look, I suppose.'

'Good—because I've been dying to look at it for ages.'

He laughed and drained his coffee. 'So this is all for your benefit, really,' he teased, and Fliss shook her head.

'Not at all. It'll just frustrate me to bits because I'd love to have the money to do it up.

It could be wonderful—and it's a fantastic investment.'

'Investment? That sounds dangerous. How much is it?'

She shrugged. 'Don't know. I don't even know the guide yet. It's up for auction.'

'Oh, no!' He threw up his hands in protest. 'No way. I couldn't do that.'

'Why? It's fun. I've bought loads of houses at auction. It can be a great idea.'

He frowned. 'Crazy woman. I always thought there was something wrong with you, I just couldn't place it.'

Fliss chuckled. 'You just don't know how to have fun.'

'Oh, I do,' he argued, his voice dropping to a rough, seductive growl that made her pulse skitter. 'I thought I'd proved that the other night. I just don't like provoking my heart condition.'

'What heart condition?' she asked, suddenly concerned. He hadn't behaved the other night as if he'd had a heart condition.

'The one I'll get if I listen to you and your wild ideas about auctions.'

'It's not wild,' she assured him, stupidly relieved that he'd only been teasing her. 'There are no unresolved legal issues, no nasty surprises—you just have to do your homework, work out your budget, set a realistic limit and stick to it.'

'All of which you can do, of course,' he said drily. 'Being a woman of so many talents.'

She just smiled smugly, and he laughed and rolled his eyes. 'You're one crazy lady, you know that?'

'This might be the only way to get something to fit your specification,' she pointed out with some truth. 'Especially if you keep looking at the million-plus ones! Do you want a house or not?'

'I'm not sure I do want one that badly,' he said, laughter in his voice. 'I feel as if you're telling me to wade through a pool full of piranhas and expecting me to trust you when you say they aren't hungry.'

'Coward,' she said, and leaving the word hanging in the air, she went out to the desk and rang her mother.

'Are you busy this afternoon?' she asked without preamble.

'Not really. I was just looking at the garden and wondering if I could be bothered to mow the lawn. Why?'

'Fancy a stroll down to the post office? The Red House is coming up for sale. I want to know who the agent is.'

'And June will know, of course,' her mother said thoughtfully. 'Well, now, it looks a nice afternoon for a little walk. I'll call you later.'

She had her answer in less than an hour, and called the agent.

'I'm going over there at five with another viewer—want to tag along?' he asked, and she arranged to be there at five-thirty, and went and found Tom.

'We're viewing it at five-thirty,' she told him, and his eyes widened.

'That was quick.'

'Speedy Gonzales, me,' she said with a grin. 'Don't get sidetracked, we'll need to leave at ten past five.'

The house terrified Tom.

The roof was full of holes, the ceilings were down in some rooms, the windows were rotten, and mod cons were notable only by their absence.

And yet Felicity was wandering round it with her eyes sparkling, excitement pouring off her in waves, and when he listened to her describing what it would be like, he could almost imagine it.

'Just picture Christmas—everyone gathered round the fire, a huge tree in the corner, and it would have to be huge, because these ceilings are about eleven or twelve feet high, and there would be holly and mistletoe from the garden draped over the windows and all round the fireplace. And you'd all be stretched out on the big comfy furniture stuffing chocolates and nuts and watching the telly—and on the floor you'd have lots of squashy cushions for the kids to lie on,' she finished, her eyes filled with sentiment. 'Oh, Tom, can't you imagine it?'

Imagine it? Dammit, he could smell it, taste it, feel the warmth of the fire and hear the crackle of the logs. And it was horribly, horribly tempting.

Too tempting. Dangerously so.

'And in here,' she went on, dragging him into what he supposed was the kitchen, 'imagine a big oil-fired range and hand-built units and a huge table in the middle, and the dogs— have you got dogs?'

'My parents have got a dog,' he told her, humouring her by playing along with the make-believe.

'The dog lying in front of the range, a cat asleep in the basket of washing—got a cat?'

His lips twitched. 'Two cats.'

'There you are, then. Four kids, two cats, the dog, your parents, the au pair—will you have an au pair?'

'Probably,' he agreed. 'Just to take the pressure off my parents in the holidays, and to escort the kids to Germany to stay with their mother every now and then.'

'All eight of you, then, all gathered round the table every evening with the animals at your feet, talking over the day, and in the summer you'd have the top of the stable door open and the sun streaming in... Tom, it would be wonderful,' she said, and he wondered if he'd imagined a slightly wistful note in her voice.

He couldn't tell, though, from her face, because she'd turned away, heading off up the back stairs for another look round the nine or so bedrooms and two bathrooms, although they were hardly worthy of the name.

'This wing would be brilliant for the au pair and the children,' she said, 'and you could have the guest rooms there, and this one would obviously be yours,' she concluded, coming to rest finally in a huge room over the drawing room.

It looked out over the formal garden at the front of the house, across the overgrown remnants of the gravel sweep that looped off the drive and had originally led to the front door.

There was hardly a trace of it now, but he could picture it, and see the garden all beautifully manicured as it had been intended.

Outside, his parents and the children were wandering around, his mother touching the plants as if she was itching to get amongst them with the secateurs, his father standing staring up at the house with the first real spark of enthusiasm he'd seen in him since his retirement, and the children—well, the children were having a wonderful time, running round the lawn chasing each other and giggling. Even Catherine, usually too busy being sophisticated to enjoy herself, was letting her hair down and having fun.

He turned and studied the room again, picturing his bed there—not the makeshift sofa bed he was sleeping on at the moment, or the bed he'd shared with Jane, but a new bed, a huge mahogany four-poster hung with pale, gauzy drapes, a bed made for loving, and sitting up in the middle of it, this amazing and vital woman who was in danger of taking over his life and his heart.

She was still talking a mile a minute, her arms waving, going on about cupboards and *en suites* and shutters and space in the room for a big old chair to cuddle up in with the little ones and read a bedtime story, and as he watched her and listened to her words, he felt a strange constriction in his chest.

She was painting a picture of the perfect family, with her an integral part of it, and she was sucking him in, dangling something in front of him that he could never have. He met her eyes, and he could see a reflection of his own fantasy in them, and he felt his heart twist with longing.

'Well?' she said, after an endless moment. 'Tom, can't you see it?'

He nodded, because he could see it, all of it, all too clearly, and without her he was afraid it wouldn't work.

And that scared him.

'Yes, I can see it,' he said. 'It's just getting there—there's so much to think about.'

'So will you think about it?' she asked, relentless. Dammit, she was like a terrier, and she wasn't going to stop until he gave in.

He scrubbed his hands through his hair. 'I need to talk to the family,' he said, stalling for time. 'It's not exactly what I had in mind.'

'Are you sure? It's what you described. Those rooms to the right of the hall would be perfect for your parents, and it's got more than enough bedrooms for all of you and the au pair, and a safe garden for the little ones—it's perfect! They'd love it, Tom. All of them. They'd be happy here.'

'It's a building site, Felicity!' he argued, hanging on like grim death to practicality while he could feel himself sliding helplessly towards the edge of a cliff, dragged along by this mad woman and aided and abetted by his faithless family. 'They don't realise what it would be like.'

'It just needs a little TLC.'

'TLC!' He thought of the enormous amount of work that even he, a rank amateur, could see was necessary, and snorted. 'You're such an optimist,' he said wryly. 'It'll need a really in-depth survey, and God only knows what that would turn up. And what about doing the work? I suppose you know a whole fleet of tried and tested men who could come in and do that?'

'Of course.'

'Of course,' he said drily, outmanoeuvred yet again by this smart-mouthed and confident young woman. 'Why did I ever doubt it?'

And then she smiled, and he felt his arguments collapsing like a house of cards, until all that was left was need, raw and urgent and in danger of overwhelming his common sense.

'It'll be OK.' She reached up and touched him, her fingers trailing over his jaw, and he turned his face into her hand and pressed a hot, hungry kiss to her palm, threading his fingers through hers and closing his eyes for a moment until he'd got his sanity back.

'What are you doing tonight?' he asked, his voice taut. 'Later on. I need to speak to my parents and get the kids to bed, but—nine-thirty? Ten? Could I come round to your house?'

'Sure. We can talk it through. I'll buy a bottle of wine,' she promised, and in her eyes was a promise of much, much more.

Suddenly ten o'clock seemed a very long way away.

CHAPTER FIVE

SHE dropped in on her mother on the way home.

'I thought I might see you,' Helen Ryman said with a smile of welcome. 'So—was it as scary as it looks?'

'Wonderful. Not scary at all, just beautiful and in desperate need of rescuing.'

'And is he interested?'

Fliss shrugged. 'I don't know. He's coming round later tonight to talk about it. It's for him and his children and his parents, so they all have to be in agreement.'

'And who is this man?' her mother asked, eyeing her with frank curiosity.

'His name's Tom Whittaker. He's a new consultant in the department. His parents live just on the edge of town—in fact, you might know them. Eileen and David Whittaker?'

'Good heavens. Of course I know them. I've known them for years. Eileen and I did a course at the local college—a little horticulture course. Heavens, that was years ago, before your father was ill. We used to play bridge with them. Nice couple.'

'They are—or they seem to be. They looked quite keen on the house. It was Tom who was panicking.'

'Wise man. I don't know how you're always so calm, the grotty old things you do up, but it always seems to work for you. How's this one going?'

'Nearly done—it's in the paper today, actually. I meant to ring the agent and warn him it isn't finished yet, but I failed. Still, I don't suppose anyone will want to view it yet, so I've probably got a few days.'

'So can I talk you into staying for supper, or do you need to rush off and finish it?'

Fliss opened her mouth to reply, but her mobile phone rang, and she pulled it out of her pocket and answered it.

It was just the call she didn't want—or did, but maybe not yet! 'Talk of the devil,' she said. 'You obviously work late.'

'Anything to serve you,' the agent said, and she could hear his smile. 'I've got a viewing for you.'

'Peter, no! I'm not ready!'

'Course you are. Finishing touches don't matter to this couple.'

'Finishing touches? It doesn't have a kitchen!'

But she couldn't convince him, and a few moments later she cut the connection and turned to her mother with a wry smile. 'Well, so much for nobody looking for a few days. That was the estate agent—someone wants to view the house. Yes, they know it isn't finished. No, they don't mind, they want to see it now. Tonight. Apparently they've seen so much dross and so many dodgy jobs they're just desperate, and he's obviously given them some flannel about me. They'll be there at eight-thirty. So, thanks, but no thanks. I'm going to have to skip supper.'

She rushed home and did her best to make it presentable. Hard, when the kitchen units were half-built and standing around the back room, the front room was stacked with furniture and the bedrooms still didn't have carpet down, but she rolled out a few rugs, pulled the kitchen units into place more or less so they could get the idea and cleaned the kitchen window and the bathroom.

It was obviously enough. Her young couple arrived early, said they loved it and the girl burst into tears. 'It's been so awful,' she explained. 'Everything's been so shoddy or badly done, and this is just lovely. I've only got two months till the baby's born, and I thought we'd never find anywhere nice to bring it home to. Thank you so much.'

And just like that, they offered the asking price, told her their money was lined up waiting, and the house was sold. They hadn't even haggled, and that meant she only had to do this one more time and she'd be able to buy a similar house without a mortgage.

Stunned, she went into the sitting room, perched on the edge of the only accessible chair and nursed a cup of tea while it sank in. Financial security, she thought. She'd be able to give up property developing and concentrate on nursing, her first and real love.

But would she want to? She loved doing this, too—loved houses, loved unravelling the layers of history in every house she'd bought, loved bringing warmth and light and feeling into each and every one of the homes she'd rescued.

Whatever, she had one more to do and she'd need to find it soon, because the young couple were in a hurry to move in before their baby was born. And that might be tricky, because she usually moved back in with her mother for the first few weeks at least, until the house was habitable and the worst was done, but now there was Tom.

If she moved back in with her mother and he was staying with his parents then there would be nowhere they could have any privacy, and there was no way she was sneaking around in hotel rooms to grab a few minutes alone with him.

Not that time alone with him was something she needed to worry about overmuch, she thought. She'd been waiting all week for him to bring the subject up, and it had taken until today for him to get round to it, and only then because she'd reached out and touched him. And even now, today, it was probably only because he wanted to talk about the house. She'd probably been imagining the look in his eyes when he'd asked what she was doing tonight, reading far too much into it.

It's only been three days, she reminded herself. It just feels like forever because you're such a sad case. And anyway, he's busy with his family. You knew he would be. You've been busy, too, you've hardly been twiddling your thumbs.

And she didn't have time to twiddle them now, because he'd be round in less than an hour. She grabbed a couple of biscuits before she had a rapid shower, and then dressed quickly in clean jeans and a jumper that had seen better days but was at least freshly washed. A quick spritz of perfume and a flick of mascara and lipstick, and there was just time to run over to the off-licence and buy a bottle of bubbly out of their chiller to celebrate her house sale before Tom arrived.

Except, of course, that he was early, and waiting on her doorstep when she arrived back, bottle in hand.

'Champagne?' he said, eyeing the bottle warily. 'I hope you're not celebrating the Red House prematurely.'

'Just a half bottle of Cava from the offie over the road, nothing so grand as the real thing,' she confessed, 'and, no, it's nothing to do with the Red House, it's my own celebration. I've sold this place.'

'What? Already? That's fantastic! I didn't even know it was on the market.'

'Nor did I till I saw it in the paper.' She grinned, opening the door and leading him in. 'I had a young couple round, desperate to see it, apparently, and they fell in love with it and want to give me loads of money. They didn't even haggle, bless them, so I thought it called for a celebration.'

'I should say so. Got any glasses?'

She laughed. 'Somewhere. I'll look, you can wrestle the cork out.'

She found them in the nick of time, just as the cork popped, and she gave a little shriek as the cold wine foamed out over her hand. They laughed together as he filled up the glasses, then, taking one from her, he raised the glass, his eyes locking with hers, and the laughter died.

'To Suffolk's sexiest and most successful property developer,' he said softly. 'Long may you prosper.'

'I'll drink to that,' she said, raising her glass. 'And to the Red House—or aren't we talking about that?'

He shook his head. 'Not now,' he said softly. 'I need to talk to the family about it at length, and think about it and let it settle before I can begin to make a decision. But here, now, we have other things to think about.'

'Such as?'

His smile was slow and lazy and sensual, and shot her pulse into orbit. 'Finding somewhere comfortable to drink this. Got any good ideas?'

Fliss sighed contentedly and turned her head so she could study Tom. He was lying beside her, stretched out on his back on top of the quilt, arms locked behind his head and a thoughtful expression on his face.

She rolled onto her front and propped herself on her elbows, bending her head to drop a kiss on his shoulder.

'Penny for them,' she said softly, and he turned his head towards her and smiled.

'I was thinking about this house, and what you're going to do now. How soon will you have to move out?'

She pulled a face. 'Soon. They've got a baby due in a couple of months, and they want it yesterday. They've got their money organised and I know their solicitor, he's fast. I'll probably be out in three or four weeks, barring hitches.'

'So what happens next? Where will you live?'

'With my mother, in Tuddingfield, until I get the next one? I don't know. She'd drive me mad if I was there more than a few weeks, but it all depends on the next house. If something comes up and it's not too bad, I could maybe live in it straight away. And that would have advantages, of course.'

'We'd have privacy, for one.'

She laughed softly. 'That was the main advantage.'

His mouth tipped into a slow, warm smile. 'Good. I'd hate to think I didn't figure in your plans.'

He shifted onto one elbow, leaning over her and running his lips slowly across her shoulder and down her back. Her eyes closed as she shut down all other senses and focussed on the sensation in her skin.

Fingertips trailed over her hip, up her spine, tangling in her hair, turning her head up to meet his face, so that those clever, clever lips could nip and nibble their way along her jaw, teasing her, dragging out the suspense until finally, finally, he claimed her mouth with his.

She turned into his arms, relishing the feel of his body, sleekly muscled, the hair rough in contrast to the satin smoothness of his skin. His thigh, hot and heavy, wedged between hers, bringing his body hard up against hers and driving all the air from her lungs.

'Felicity,' he groaned, and then without hesitation her body was welcoming his, matching every touch, every thrust, every breath and heartbeat until finally, when she thought she'd die if she had to wait another moment, she was falling over the edge and tumbling headlong, freefalling back to earth in the safety of his arms.

He collapsed against her, his chest heaving, his heart hammering against her ribs in time with her own, and then gradually, as their hearts slowed, he lifted his head and stared down into her eyes.

For an age he said nothing, just looked at her, then still in silence he rolled to his side, taking her with him, and cradled her against his heart. Their bodies were still locked together, so close that she didn't know where she ended and he began, as if they were truly a part of each other.

They didn't speak. Words were superfluous. Instead their bodies spoke for them, their hands moving slowly, lovingly over each other, little touches, tender gestures. Cherishing.

Then finally he sighed and kissed her softly, and she felt him distance himself. 'I have to go,' he said.

'I know.'

She didn't try and stop him. There was no point. He had a family waiting for him, children who'd need him in the morning, and she had a kitchen to fit tomorrow and carpets to order and the estate agent and solicitor to phone.

Reality was crowding back, and she didn't try and stop it. She needed it, needed to remember what it was all about, what they were doing here together.

And playing happy families wasn't it.

'We didn't finish the fizzy.'

'Don't worry, I've got a stopper. It'll keep. Anyway, you're driving.'

She watched him dress, then pulled on her robe and went downstairs with him, pausing by the front door to reach up and press another slow, lingering kiss to his lips. 'Thank you for tonight,' she whispered.

A muscle flexed in his jaw. 'Don't thank me,' he said gruffly. 'You've given me so much—warmth, friendship, a chance to be the other side of myself. And that's just for starters. That's without the fun, the laughter, the sheer joy of being with you. I can't explain—there just aren't words.'

She pressed a finger to his lips. 'Then don't try and find them. I understand. Now go. I need my beauty sleep.' She kissed him again, then opened the door and waved him down the path before going back up to her rumpled bed.

The wine needed capping, but she wasn't sure she could be bothered for such a small dribble. It was probably flat by now, anyway, and she wasn't a great wine drinker. Not a great anything drinker, really, unless you counted tea.

Now, that sounded good. Tea, and a hot bath. Together. She scooped up the wine bottle and glasses, and went back downstairs to put the kettle on. She'd drink the tea while she wallowed, then get back into bed and sleep until she woke naturally.

It had been ages since she'd had a lie-in. She'd been up at the crack of dawn for weeks, getting the house done, but now it was almost there and she reckoned she'd earned it.

She might even go for broke and have breakfast in bed—and then she'd do the kitchen.

Or maybe she'd just get up and finish it, and then she could really relax.

'Done your kitchen?'

She jumped, startled by Tom's voice in her ear, and she shut her locker door and turned to him, her hand over her heart, laughter bubbling up inside her.

'Yes, thank you for asking. I've just got one or two bits left to do, but I need to borrow some muscles. I don't suppose you're up for it?'

'Me?' He threw up his hands in horror. 'I don't do muscles.'

'Well, now, I've seen them, so I know that's a lie,' she said softly, her mouth twitching with laughter. 'Try again.'

'I'm busy?'

She snorted. 'Not good enough. I need half an hour—an hour, tops. And I could feed you then. I'd have the facilities.'

He tipped his head on one side, studying her thoughtfully for a moment, then sighed. 'I'm not going to get away with saying no, am I?' he murmured.

'No.'

'When?'

'Whenever you can. It's just to hold the wall cupboards while I mark the fixings.'

'And you'll feed me?'

She nodded.

'How about Friday or Saturday night? The kids are all going to their maternal grandparents for the weekend, being picked up straight from school, and my parents are going down to visit friends in Chichester on Saturday and staying the night. I'm on call, but I might be able to sneak a few hours.'

'I'm on an early on Friday and a late on Saturday, so Friday would be better if you want a meal. And if your kids are away, you could stay the night,' she suggested, wondering if that was going beyond the bounds of his carefully orchestrated rule book, but he just smiled, his eyes warming.

'And you can cook me breakfast. I'll tell my parents I'm staying at the hospital to be closer.'

'Do you have to tell them anything?' she asked, but he just chuckled and raised an eyebrow.

'Put yourself in my shoes,' he said quietly. 'What would you tell your mother—I'm working at the hospital so I'll be staying there, or

I'm going to visit my new lover and having wild sex all night?'

'Who said anything about wild sex?' she said, ignoring the little surge of interest from her body. 'I thought we were talking about kitchen units.'

'Of course. Silly me. Or I could stay on Saturday night and nobody will be any the wiser.'

'Aren't you dog sitting?'

He shook his head. 'No, they're taking the dog. The other couple are great walkers, so they're going out on the Downs if the weather's nice. My father can't walk all that well, so he takes the car, has a nice little drive around and meets them at the pub at the other end.'

'Sounds perfect,' she said with a laugh. 'And you get the night off.'

'Except I'm on call, so your kitchen might not even happen. Why don't I pop round later tonight? Then we'll have the weekend free to do whatever we want.'

She nodded, a little ripple of anticipation running through her. 'I'm on a late today, so I won't be home till after eight.'

'And I'll be tied up with bedtime until after nine, so I'll make it later—say, ten?'

'Sure. Any more thoughts on the Red House, by the way?'

His mouth tipped into a wry smile. 'I wondered when you were going to ask.'

'I was trying not to nag.'

'You don't need to—I've got a surveyor onto it, and I've spoken to the agent about putting in an offer and buying it prior to the auction. He's coming back to me on it.'

'Wow! So you really are serious.' She felt a shiver of excitement, and he laughed and shook his head.

'You love it, don't you? I feel sick just thinking about it. I must have been crazy to let you talk me into it.'

'What's she talked you into?' Matt said, coming up behind them and putting a hand on each of their shoulders. 'Am I missing something here?'

'Don't ever mention to this woman that you're looking for a house,' Tom said, deadpan, while Fliss chuckled.

'A house?' Matt said with a grin. 'You told her you were looking for a house? Fatal mistake. I could have warned you about that. Listen, if we're all done here, I wonder if you could spare me a minute? I'd like a second opinion. I've got a tricky case, it might be Marfan's syndrome.'

He took Tom away, and Fliss headed out of the staffroom, humming softly to herself. Just ten hours to go and he'd be coming round, she thought. She could hardly wait.

Meg paused as she was passing and grinned at her.

'You sound happy. Good weekend?'

'Great weekend. Sold my house, fitted the kitchen and even got some sleep.'

'Good. So you'll be nice and fresh to deal with Mr Cordy. His finger's gone septic.'

'Cordy?'

'The guy with the broken nail who made such a fuss when we had that big RTA? He's back—and he ain't happy. Cubicle three.'

'Oh, joy,' Fliss sighed, and arming herself with a good deep breath and a spray-on smile, she flicked open the curtain and went in.

'Mr Cordy.'

'Oh, it's you. It's gone septic. Look. I could sue you lot for that.'

She peered at the hugely swollen finger and frowned. 'That doesn't look good. Perhaps it would have been a good idea to have waited and had it treated properly, instead of tearing off the nail and asking for a plaster. I understand that's what happened?'

'Well, I wasn't going to be seen for hours—and anyway, it was only a nail.'

'Well, now it's a septic nail,' she pointed out, and turning his hand over, she ran her finger up the red line that extended up his forearm. 'And see this? This is infection tracking up your arm. You should have gone to see your doctor days ago.'

'Well, it was the weekend. They don't work weekends, and I couldn't get an appointment this morning. And anyway, I wanted you to see what you'd done.'

'What I'd done?' She raised her eyebrows and stood back, looking at him questioningly. 'I don't think I did anything, Mr Cordy. I didn't get a chance. If I'd been able to treat it, you would have had a course of antibiotics and a proper sterile dressing, not just a plaster.'

'So why wasn't I given that?'

'Because you refused to wait?'

'Life's too short.'

'Well, yours could be, if we don't get this properly treated, because you've got blood poisoning now, Mr Cordy, so I suggest you sit right there until I get a doctor to look at you, and then we'll decide what's the best course of action.'

She opened the curtain, to find Tom standing there, his mouth twitching.

'Is that who I think it is?' he murmured, and she nodded.

'Mr Cordy.'

'Of the broken nail.'

'Indeed. He's got a nasty red line tracking up his arm, and he's threatening legal action.'

'Oh, nice. We'll see about that.' He swished the curtain out of the way and went in, and Fliss nearly choked on a laugh. She didn't like the look of that smile at *all*.

'Mr Cordy!' Tom said cheerfully. 'I understand your finger's become infected.'

'That's right—look at it.'

He tutted at the proffered digit. 'Oh, dear, very nasty. Pity you didn't stay and let us treat it, but that's all right. I think we might be able to save the arm—what do you think, Sister Ryman? Any hope?'

Fliss didn't think any such thing. Fliss was busy trying not to choke on her laughter.

'Well, it might be touch and go,' she managed after a moment spent apparently examining the finger.

'You're joking!' Mr Cordy said, looking panic-stricken, and Tom relented.

'Fortunately for you, yes. Mr Cordy, you have been lucky, we can easily treat this, but I must point out that it would never have happened if it had been properly treated in the first place, and the reason it wasn't is not our fault.

In future, it might be as well to allow the professionals to do their job instead of doing it for them. Now, are you allergic to penicillin?'

'Um—no, I don't think so,' Mr Cordy muttered, looking suitably chastened, and Fliss stifled a smile.

'Good.' He glanced down at the finger, turned the hand over and reached for the notes. 'OK, Sister, if you could debride it and dress it, give him a penicillin injection and this prescription...' he scribbled on the pad and tore it off, handing it to her '...and I think Mr Cordy will live. Thank you, Sister. Mr Cordy.'

And he walked out, leaving Fliss on the verge of laughter and their thwarted patient in a sulk.

She dressed his finger, gave him the injection and the prescription and sent him on his way.

'Give you any more grief?' Tom asked her, passing her in the corridor a moment later, and she chuckled.

'Only for being a sadist when I cleaned it up. I don't think we'll be seeing him again, thank goodness. What a difficult man.'

'Stupid man. Fancy letting it get that bad before he came back. Right, I'm glad you're free, you can give me a hand with another lulu. There's a man been admitted with a bottle in his rectum—and before you ask, you don't want to know.'

'On a Monday?' she said, her smile refusing to be held back. 'That's normally a Saturday night thing.'

'That's how long it's been there—and he's getting very unhappy about it.'

'I'm sure,' she said, her mouth twitching. 'It must be a right royal pain in the—'

'Indeed,' Tom said, and his eyes sparkled with laughter. 'I wish I knew why people have this crazy urge to stick foreign bodies in their orifices. If it isn't this sort of thing, it's kids with peas up their noses.'

Fliss chuckled. 'Tell me about it. Oh, well, it livens things up a bit.'

'Oh, absolutely. The day just gets better, doesn't it? Well, come on, let's get him sorted out and on his way so we can get on with something useful, like lunch—if it doesn't put me right off my food.'

Grinning, she followed him down the corridor.

Tom got the surveyor's preliminary report on Thursday, together with a rough breakdown of the likely costs of essential work.

'What the hell does essential mean?' he asked his mother and father, but they shook their heads.

'No idea,' his father said. 'You need to ask an expert.'

And so he rang her, the woman he was beginning to think of as his resident expert, and asked her.

'Oh, I think that needs dinner,' she said. 'And I'd like to take a look at the surveyor's report before I can tell you the answer.'

'So come round. We haven't eaten—Mum's made some chicken thing. Knowing her, it'll feed an army. I've got something to ask you, anyway.'

There was a little pause, then he almost felt her make the decision.

'OK, you've convinced me. I haven't had real food for ages. I'll see you in a few minutes.'

He felt his shoulders drop, and realised he'd been holding his breath. Crazy.

'See you soon,' he said, and resisted the urge to tell her to drive carefully, to take care, or any of the other proprietorial things he found he wanted to say.

Frowning, he put the phone down and sat for a second, deep in thought, then went and broke the news to his mother that she had another mouth to feed.

'Oh, lovely. I thought she was such a charming girl,' his father said, but his mother just smiled knowingly and threw a few more cherry tomatoes in the salad.

Damn.

'I'm going round to Zoe's,' Catherine said, and he was on the point of agreeing when he caught himself.

'I don't think so. Grannie's cooked you supper.'

'That's OK, I'm not hungry.'

'I didn't ask if you were hungry. You don't just tell us you're going out, you ask if you can, and you know you don't go out except to school functions during the week.'

'But it's about homework.'

'What homework?'

'Chemistry,' she said, and he raised an eyebrow.

'And I can't help you with it?'

'What do you know about chemistry?'

He rolled his eyes. 'Oh, sorry, I forgot, chemistry was only invented after I left school.'

'Dad, things have changed,' she said patiently, as if he were an idiot child, and he took a nice, deep, steadying breath.

'Indeed. Children used to be polite. They did as they were told, and they didn't answer back to their elders. And they didn't wear make-up to school!' he added to her departing back.

The door slammed, and he winced, but his mother laughed.

'She's so like your sister—and don't tell me children didn't answer back. You, young man, had an answer for everything!'

'That's because I was naturally brilliant,' he said drily, and started to lay the table. He hadn't even finished when Catherine came back in.

'Right. I've finished my homework. Can I go now, please?' she asked, her tone only slightly patronising.

He was going to say no, but then he thought how worried he'd be about her not making friends at her new school.

'Is her mother there?'

'Yes. She's said it's OK.'

'And where is this?'

'Only the next road—Kingsbury Avenue. Number eight. It's, like, two minutes' walk, Dad, and it's hardly the red light district.'

He didn't want to know what his daughter knew about red light districts! 'All right, then, but back by nine,' he said, conceding on this one occasion. 'And have your mobile with you. And you go straight there and straight back. You aren't going anywhere else, is that clear?'

'As crystal,' she said, her voice bored. 'You all finished now with the lectures?'

'I should thrash your backside,' he said mildly. 'Say sorry to Grannie for not letting her know about missing supper.'

'Sorry, Grannie,' she said dutifully, but she did sound a little penitent and genuine, so he let it go. One small victory at a time, he thought, and after a hard day at the hospital, frankly, he'd settle for anything he could get.

Peace and quiet would be nice.

Then Michael burst in, followed by Abby in tears, and he realised that quiet was a forlorn hope, and peace wasn't far behind it.

CHAPTER SIX

'SO, WHAT was it you wanted to ask me yester-day?'

They'd discussed the house over supper, torn the surveyor's report to bits and put it together again, and then before he'd been able to say anything he'd had a call from Catherine to pick her up from her friend's house, because it had started raining.

So Fliss had gone home to get an early night because she had to be at work at seven the following morning, and now they were lying in her bed, Friday finally over and the kids off Tom's hands for the weekend, and her curiosity would wait no longer.

'It's about the house,' he began.

'I rather thought it might be,' Fliss said wryly.

She tipped her head on one side and studied him. If ever a man had an agenda, it was this one, and she had a funny feeling she was on it. She just couldn't work out how. 'So?' she said warily. 'What's the problem? You need to get quotes first.'

'Mmm. And if I buy it—assuming I can get it for a reasonable price at the auction—I'll need someone who knows what they're doing to supervise it all.'

'And you want me to suggest a project manager?' she asked. 'I don't know any.'

'Not exactly.' He broke off, turning towards her, his eyes searching her face. 'Felicity, I can't do it alone. I need your help with this,' he said persuasively. 'We make a good team. We work well together.'

'Well, I'll help you, Tom. Of course I'll help you. I know all sorts of people who won't rip you off, and I can tell you where to source things.'

'You don't understand,' he said, shaking his head. 'I want more than that. I want you there with me, working alongside me, making it all happen. I want you to be my project manager, Felicity. I want you to run the show.'

She stared at him, momentarily stunned by his request. 'Wow,' she said, when she could get her mouth to work again. 'Project manager? I've never done anything on this scale, Tom. Are you sure?'

'As sure as I can be. I trust you.'

'More fool you.'

She chewed her lip, considering not just the enormity of the task, but what it would involve. Most particularly, the way it would throw her and Tom together. She'd have to build him a dream, one she'd have no part of, and already, even after such a short time, she knew the impact that could have on her.

Heavens, she got involved enough doing up a simple little house when she had no idea who it was for, and now she'd got her buyers she'd been thinking of that young woman preparing food in the kitchen she'd fitted, glancing down at her baby on the floor she'd laid, smiling at it, bathing it upstairs in the bath she'd installed—and this was a woman she'd met once. Once!

How on earth could she hope to keep any kind of emotional distance from the job if she was doing it for Tom and his family? She must be nuts to even give the thought houseroom!

She opened her mouth to say no, but, as if he'd anticipated her answer, he laid a finger over her lips and smiled.

'Don't answer yet. I don't want you saying no and then regretting it, or saying yes and then bottling out halfway through. Think about it. Take your time. There's no immediate rush.'

What on earth was he thinking about? Asking Fliss to help him with the house was crazy. He'd vowed to keep her away from his family, to keep this part of his life separate from the other part, and here he was, not only dragging her into the very creation of his home, but inviting her to take control of it! He must be nuts!

Until yesterday she'd only ever met Catherine and his parents twice, and that fleetingly. She'd never even set eyes on the other

three children except while they'd been viewing the house. And here he was, opening doors
that were better left firmly closed, drawing her
in, involving her in the deepest way with the
realisation of the dream she'd painted so elo-
quently for him as they'd walked around the
empty, echoing shell and she'd filled it with
images of warmth and laughter.

He couldn't believe it. He'd been so adamant about never getting involved with a
woman ever again, and yet here he was, asking
her to create a home for his family after only
a fortnight or so.

She'd be there all the time, popping in and
out when she wasn't at work, delving into
every nook and cranny—and her personality
would be stamped all over it.

'Are you sure?' she said doubtfully, as if
she'd realised that he wasn't, not in the least.
'I mean—it's a bit sudden. I might screw it up
completely. You hardly know me.'

He laughed, the sound slightly strained to
his ears. 'I wouldn't say that. I probably know
you a lot better than I'd get to know any other

project manager. Besides, how well do I need to know you? It's not as if I'm asking you to marry me!'

A look of shock appeared on her face. 'I should hope not!' she replied instantly. 'I'd far rather take on your house than your four kids, no matter how delightful they might be!'

She rolled away from him, propping herself up against the headboard and staring out of the window, her face unreadable. 'How long have I got?'

'Got?'

'To think about your proposition—or do I mean proposal?' she said drily, and he felt something akin to panic flutter in his chest.

Oh, lord. Why had he mentioned marriage? Why had the subject even arisen, and why the *hell* did it suddenly sound so tempting? Idiot, he told himself furiously. Back off. Slow down. You can't afford to get so deeply involved, and you know she doesn't want to. You heard her reply—she sounded horrified at the very idea. And she certainly doesn't want the kids, she wasn't joking about that bit.

That's the second woman in a row who's felt like that about them. You can't do that to them.

So what should he do? Walk away? Have nothing more to do with this tempting, beautiful woman who turned his guts inside out?

And then he'd be alone again.

The thought was unbearable.

Oh, hell. He groaned inwardly. He was in deep—deeper than he'd realised, deeper than he'd ever meant to get, and suddenly he felt as if he was running in quicksand.

'Take as long as you want,' he said, and he found himself wishing she'd take long enough to talk herself out of it.

Or did he?

She couldn't believe she was so stupid. When Tom had said that, she'd felt a second of crushing disappointment, and why? She didn't want to marry him, a divorced man with four children and a chip on his shoulder the size of the house! She knew that! And it wasn't even as if he was asking her.

But somehow, when the word 'marry' had leapt out of the conversation and clubbed her over the head, it had opened her eyes to her true feelings, and now she was reeling with shock.

Because, perversely, although someone else's kids were way down her agenda, and four of them were off the scale, somehow she felt—what? Cheated?

Ridiculous.

The silly thing was, if he'd asked her while they were sitting in the staffroom at work she wouldn't have reacted as she had, she would have laughed. But somehow, lying here in bed with him when he'd just made love to every inch of her with such tenderness and care— somehow that just made it different.

It didn't change anything, only her perception of it, but that was enough to throw her completely.

'I'll pay you, of course,' he carried on, ramming home the fact that it was only a business arrangement. 'Just name your price. I know you won't cheat me. And I realise it's a hell of a job, and you won't be able to do a house of your own at the same time, so I'll factor your loss of profit into the equation.'

Loss of profit was the least of her worries, but he was right, it was a huge job, far bigger than anything she'd tackled, and no doubt that would dawn on her later, but just now she was busy trying not to cry with shock and frustration and disappointment, and something else that was just beginning to register.

'You're right, I need to think about it,' she said, wondering how on earth she managed to sound so normal when her world was tumbling down around her ears—because in the course of the last few minutes, she'd realised something fundamental and earth-shattering that had changed everything.

She was in love with him.

Deeply, totally, go-to-the-ends-of-the-earth in love with him, and to work on the house for him, to create a home for him and his family that she would never share—that was going to tear her apart. And yet how could she let anyone else do it?

'What if I say no?' she asked, testing his reaction, pushing him, needing to know how important she was to him before she committed herself.

He shrugged. 'I don't know. It's up to you, but I hope you won't. I know nothing about this business, it's a huge step into the unknown for me, and I'll need someone I can rely on on my side every inch of the way. I just hope you don't regret it, if you decide to do it.'

And because she had no choice, because her stupid, stupid heart had given itself to him for ever, she plastered a brave smile on her face and turned to him and said, 'Of course I'll do it—if you get the house. There's no guarantee you will.'

And hanging onto that thought was possibly the only thing that would save her sanity.

She had plenty of time over the weekend to consider his suggestion, and all the possible ramifications of it, and it didn't do anything for her peace of mind.

Tom was on call, and when he was summoned to the hospital shortly after six on Saturday morning, Fliss took advantage of the glorious weather and her late start to go outside and finish tidying the garden and clearing away the aftermath of the building work.

It was an absolutely gorgeous day, and while she worked, she thought of the little family who would be playing here in this garden, the baby who would sleep out here in his or her pram under the little apple tree, then next summer learn to walk out here on the soft, yielding grass.

And she was fantasising again, painting pictures of happy families to torture herself with.

So, instead of torturing herself with that, she tortured herself with thoughts of Tom and his children in the garden at the Red House, and gathered round the fire, and seated at the long refectory table in the kitchen she'd created for them, and that was even worse.

If she had any sense she wouldn't take it on, she thought, but she knew the answer to that already, had already committed herself. She could only hope it wouldn't happen, but that wasn't fair. They needed a home, somewhere to settle and heal from the battering of a broken marriage, and if she could help them find that peace, then she'd do it.

She just hoped the cost to her sanity wouldn't be too high a price to pay.

She looked round the garden, clear now of all the last bits and pieces, the shrubs and perennials just bursting with life, and she nodded with satisfaction. They'd have a nice garden here now to complement the house, somewhere safe for the baby—and there she went again!

She got to her feet, brushed down her jeans and went in for a quick shower. She had twenty minutes before she had to leave, and it would take all of that to get the dirt out of her hands.

By the time she got to work at twelve, her fingers tingling from the scrubbing she'd given them, Tom had been in the department for nearly six hours and was slouched in the staff lounge with a coffee in hand.

'Had a nice lie-in?' he asked with a wry smile, and she raised an eyebrow.

'Hardly. Been finishing off the garden, since you seem to think you're going to have me tied up in the Red House.'

'Now, there's an interesting prospect,' he said, his smile widening, and she rolled her eyes and dumped her bag in her locker.

'So, what's going on? You don't look exactly busy. Afraid I'd give you a job if you came back to mine?'

'Hardly!' he said with a chuckle. 'I've just stopped for a coffee. It's been hell. There was a spate of DIY and gardening accidents, people with bad hearts overdoing the digging to get their vegetables in and then, of course, sunburn will follow, won't it? It's funny, people sit on their bottoms for months on end, and at the first sign of decent weather they all rush out and damage themselves! Crazy.'

'And you were involved because...?'

He gave her a wry grin. 'I know. There was a bad burns case this morning early, and I just sort of ended up staying. You know how it is.'

'Absolutely—which is why I steer clear of the place unless I'm on duty.' She checked her watch, and headed for the door. 'Back on the treadmill. Are you going home now?'

His smile was wry. 'Trying to get rid of me?'

'No—but your SHO might be. Perhaps he wants to make his mistakes alone.'

Tom chuckled. 'I doubt it. He seemed quite happy to have me here this morning—but you're right. I might as well save my energy for when I'm really needed.'

And, of course, just because he said that, Meg stuck her head round the door and sighed with relief.

'Glad you're still here. We've got an acute abdomen just come in, the new house officer is out of his depth. Would you mind, Tom?'

'Of course not,' he said, getting to his feet and shooting Fliss a rueful smile. 'Want to join me? I'd like you on board for this one if possible.'

'I'd better find out what else is in store. I'll help you if I can—depends who's there.' She followed him up the corridor. The patient was in the trolley bay, having been admitted by ambulance, and he was curled on his side and sweating profusely. Meg was already back with him, bending over him, wiping his mouth and taking away a paper sick bowl, while Steve scribbled furiously in the notes.

Fliss caught Meg's eye. 'Want me to take over from you here?' she asked, and Meg nodded.

'I was in the middle of something, but I had to stop. I'll get back to them if you're happy.' She put the bowl down. 'He's all yours. Mr Carter, I'm handing you over to Fliss. She'll take care of you now.'

Fliss smiled to herself. Meg hated vomiting patients, and she'd hand them over at the slightest opportunity. Unfortunately Fliss didn't like them either, and today was no exception.

'You're going to owe me for this,' she told Tom softly, and he chuckled.

'So sue me,' he said, and bent over the patient. 'Hello, Mr Carter. My name's Tom

Whittaker. I gather you're not feeling too great.'

'Sick,' the man said, swallowing convulsively. 'Hurts.'

'OK. Where does it hurt?'

The man waved vaguely at his upper abdomen, then retched again.

'And what came first, the pain or the vomiting?'

'Pain.'

Tom nodded again. 'OK, Steve, what have you done so far?'

Steve looked at the notes in his hand. 'Brief history, clinic examination and set up the drip. Normal saline for the shock but we've sent blood for FBC, U&E, blood sugar and amylase.'

'Good. Any thoughts?'

'Um—looks like peritonitis. Abdomen's rigid, patient's shocked, severe pain.'

Tom nodded. 'Cause of the peritonitis?'

Steve looked blank. 'Haven't got that far.'

Tom had, though, Fliss realised when he next spoke.

'Mr Carter, I see you've got a wrist support on. Have you been taking any painkillers recently?'

'Oh—yes. Something I got from the doctor. Dic-something. I've got carpal tunnel syndrome.'

'Diclofenac? Volterol?'

'That's it. Been taking it for a week or two.'

Tom nodded. 'Right. Well, I think it might have caused a hole in your stomach, which is what's giving you so much pain. I'm going to give you some morphine to ease it, get an X-ray to look for gas in your abdomen, we'll start you on antibiotics in your drip and we'll get you up to Theatre so they can fix you, but the first thing we're going to do is get a tube into your stomach to empty it, which should stop the nausea for you and help us get a better idea of what's going on in there.'

He turned to Meg. 'Can you do me a nasogastric tube and I'll get some morphine into him. Mr Carter, are you allergic to penicillin?'

But Mr Carter was past caring, and was busy emptying his stomach yet again.

'His wife's out in the waiting room,' Steve said. 'She might know.'

He went off to check, leaving Fliss to put in the nasogastric tube.

Funny, normally it didn't worry her at all, but today it made her feel a little queasy. She was relieved when Mr Carter was settled on pain relief, the probable diagnosis was confirmed by the X-ray showing free gas in his abdomen, and he was whisked away to Theatre.

She stripped off her gloves and plastic apron, and Tom shot her a funny look.

'You OK? You looked a little green around the gills for a minute.'

She shrugged. 'Sometimes it just gets to me. Right, I suppose I ought to find out where else I'm needed. Preferably a nice tidy fracture and no retching.'

Tom chuckled. 'Absolutely. Right, Steve, let's go through that.'

She left them to it, finding Meg and establishing what was going on before starting on her next patient.

'Thanks for that,' Meg said with a relieved smile. 'You know it always makes me heave. You're a star.'

'You owe me,' she said grimly. 'Right, what's next?'

'You've got a choice,' Meg said. 'You can suture a hand, or glue the scalp of an addict who's had a bit too much to drink.'

'I'll suture,' she said quickly, and Meg grinned.

'How did I know you'd say that? OK, he's in cubicle two.'

And so the day proceeded, until finally it was eight o'clock and she could go home. She felt incredibly tired, but of course with Tom staying last night she hadn't had much sleep, and it had been a busy shift if not particularly dramatic, hard on the heels of all that gardening.

And now she had to go home and cook.

'How about dinner?'

Tom fell into step beside her, close enough that she could feel his warmth, but not quite touching. Not in the hospital, in front of their colleagues, who were all desperate romantics and serial matchmakers.

'Dinner?'

'Mmm. We could go out, or if you'd rather not we could grab something instant on the way home.'

'Or we could have beans on toast and lie in front of the telly and do nothing.'

He grinned. 'Beans on toast sounds good to me. Let's go.'

And after they'd eaten, she curled up on the sofa, her head on his shoulder, and slept until he woke her and carried her up to bed.

By the time the day of the auction arrived at the end of the following week, Fliss's little army of tradesmen had been in and scratched their heads and submitted quotes for the work.

Some had come in over the surveyor's estimate, others below, but the broad ballpark figure was similar, and so Tom reluctantly found himself taking the day off and going to the auction, Fliss firmly anchored to his side.

'I can't do this without you,' he told her. 'I want you here.'

'I'll be here. I want to bid for a bungalow, anyway. I'm going to be out of my house in a fortnight now, and I've got nowhere to go. The bungalow looks possible.'

He stared at her. 'You amaze me. Here I am, terrified, and you've only just bothered to mention it.'

'But it's not my dream, so it doesn't matter,' she told him, and wondered if that was a rather revealing thing to say.

Of course.

'So, what is your dream?' he asked, and because she couldn't tell him the truth, she just shrugged.

'I don't know. Something old and rambling.'

'Like the Red House?'

Exactly like the Red House. Damn.

'Shh. Look, it's starting. Concentrate, see how it goes with the other properties.'

'I can't. I'm going to be sick,' he told her candidly, and she laughed and took pity on him and squeezed his hand, under the cover of her long cardigan. She was standing in front of him, right at the back of the auction room, so they could keep an eye on the proceedings and check out the opposition.

She didn't get the bungalow. Bidding was too brisk, and she shook her head and withdrew once she'd reached her limit.

'Wow. You'd better keep an eye on me, I won't have that much discipline,' he murmured in her ear.

Nor will I, she thought. Not for that house, the one I've dreamed about for years, the one I've always loved and wanted, the one you want me to turn into a safe haven for your family.

'Tell me your limit again,' she said, but he just smiled.

'Just get it for me, Felicity,' he said. 'The money doesn't matter.'

She felt her eyes widen, but he was the boss. It was his money.

'I think you should bid.'

'No. You do it. I can't trust myself.'

She wasn't sure he could trust her either, but in the end he took it out of her hands, when the bidding went crazy and she was about to bottle out, and put in one last, final bid.

And that was it. The hammer fell, and the house was his, and forgetting any idea of discretion or propriety or dignity, he picked her up and whirled her round in his arms, laughing, until the auction house official came and tapped him on the arm and brought him down to earth.

'Sign here, sir,' he said, and that was that.

They had a party at the house that evening, Tom and his parents and the children, and Felicity, of course, without whom he wouldn't have dared to do this crazy and foolish thing.

They strolled through the house together, listening to the sound of the children running through the upstairs rooms, their feet drumming on the bare boards, and he turned to Felicity and gave her a wry grin.

'So—tell me again I've done the right thing,' he said, and she laughed and told him not to worry.

Worry? He didn't know where to start worrying! 'I take it the kids won't actually come through the floorboards?' he asked, listening to the sound of them crashing about overhead, and she shook her head.

'Don't think so,' she replied, which didn't do a lot for his confidence.

The only part of it that didn't seem too bad was the little wing his parents would have, the area the old ladies had retreated to from the rot and damp, and there, with the evening sun coming in through the open windows and the sound of the birds in the background, he could actually imagine that it would be all right.

'This bit's really in very good condition,' Felicity said, wandering around craning her neck at the ceilings and the window-frames. 'You could live in it now.'

'Or you could,' he said, the idea suddenly coming to him. 'How about it? You didn't get the bungalow, you haven't got anywhere to go—how about here? You'd be on the spot for the job, which would surely make it easier, you wouldn't have to worry about doing two places at once, and,' he added, his voice dropping to a soft murmur, 'we'd have some privacy.'

For a moment he thought she'd say no, refuse his offer, but it did make sense for all sorts of reasons, not least the privacy one.

The only problem was, she'd be living here, in his dream home, and yet not living here, not really, just passing through—so near and yet so far.

He must have been mad to ask her.

'I'll think about it,' she said, but her words mocked her with a hollow ring, because she already knew the answer. Of course she'd live there. It solved so many things—supervision of the job, solving her accommodation problem, not to mention the privacy thing—and yet it was absolutely the last thing she wanted to do.

She moved in two weeks later, handing over the keys of her house to the sweet young couple who'd bought it from her, so full of hope and happiness and the boundless optimism of youth, and for the first time ever she felt a pang of sadness.

'I hope you're really happy here,' she said, and then, impulsive as ever, she kissed them both and wished them luck with the baby and drove away, her eyes filled with silly, silly tears, because it had suddenly dawned on her that she was homeless.

What a strange thought. She'd done this so many times, but somehow she'd put a part of her heart into that little house. Was it because of Tom? Because they'd made memories there?

Made love, so many countless ways, so many times, so tenderly?

She'd been happy there, she realised, for the past few weeks. Truly happy, for the first time in ages, and it was because of Tom, because she'd been living in cloud-cuckoo-land.

And now she was going to be living in the Red House, and moving out of that when it was done would be much, much worse.

Whatever had she taken on?

CHAPTER SEVEN

IT WAS amazing how quickly everything got torn to bits, Tom thought. One minute it was a tired, sad old house, the next—well, the next defied description.

He was walking round staring at the shell of his home in horrified fascination when Felicity came in with a man he vaguely recognised.

'Remember Bill?' she said. 'He fell off his stilts. He's going to do the plastering for you.'

'Bill—I do remember. Good to see you again. How's the leg?'

Bill pulled a face and looked down at his cast, much scribbled on and grubby—and also, if Tom wasn't very much mistaken, daubed with pink plaster. 'Oh, you know—bit of a pain every now and then, but not too bad. It hasn't held me up a lot.'

'I don't think I want to hear that,' Tom said with a wince. 'How long is it now? Only five weeks or so?'

'Something like that,' Bill agreed cheerfully. 'Don't worry, your Fliss here's already choked me off for doing too much.'

His Fliss? *His* Fliss? He decided that was best ignored, and he moved swiftly on. 'So, Bill, are you going to be able to turn this wreck into a home for me and my children?' he asked, and Bill laughed.

'This is nothing, Doc. You wait till they really get started.'

Tom wondered if he had gone as white as he felt, because Felicity—*his Fliss*, indeed—took one look at him and grinned. 'Now, Bill, don't frighten him. He's finding it hard enough watching me trash his investment without you winding him up. Anyway, you've got a house to look at and a job to quote me for, so let's press on. I've got to be at work in an hour.'

Well, that answered that question, Tom thought, and went outside and wandered aimlessly around the garden. The children were in Germany visiting their mother, because it was half-term week, and so he'd volunteered to work the weekend. So now he had a day off in the middle of the week, and he'd thought he'd spend it down here, looking round the house, talking to Felicity about it.

He'd even checked her shift to be sure, but now he'd discovered she was working today after all, and so his plans for the afternoon were effectively scuppered.

She appeared by his side moments later, tilting her head on one side and screening her eyes from the sun as she squinted up at him. 'You OK?' she asked, and he smiled ruefully.

'I thought you were supposed to be off this afternoon.'

'Sorry. I had to change my shift. I'm only doing a half-shift, though, to cover Angie's dental appointment. I'm off this evening. Why don't you come over? I'll cook something— salad or something.'

'You'll cook salad? This I have to see,' he teased, and she grinned and he felt his heart ease a little. 'What time?'

'Five-thirty?'

He nodded, suddenly much more cheerful. 'I'll look forward to it.'

'Good. There's something I've got to talk to you about, anyway. And in the meantime, there are some drawings that need approval on the table in my office. Go and have a look and I'll see you later. I've got to go to work.'

She left him, fluttering her fingers in a little wave—a microwave, she called it—and left him smiling.

The day was going OK until someone threw up in front of her.

'Sorry, Meg, can you take over?' Fliss gasped, running out of the cubicle. Dashing into the loo, she dropped onto the floor and lost her lunch down the pan.

Shaken, stunned, she sat back on her heels, dabbing at her mouth with a tissue and staring blankly at the wall. Not another bug! She hadn't been ill for ages, and now she'd been ill twice in a few weeks!

Great.

She dragged herself to her feet, flushed the loo and rinsed her mouth over the basin. There was a water fountain in there, and she drank a few mouthfuls of cold water, then splashed some over her face and neck to cool it.

That was it. It was the heat. It couldn't be another bug. Nobody else had gone down with anything.

'You all right?'

She stared at Meg, then shook her head and pulled herself together. 'Yeah—yes, I'm fine. Just a bit sick. Must be the heat.'

'Maybe,' Meg agreed, but she looked doubtful.

'Oh, well, back to work,' she said, dredging up a bright smile. 'I'm starving, actually. I wonder if it's just hunger? I only had a little bit of lunch.'

'So go and have something.'

'I'm only on a half-shift, I can't really have a break.'

'Nonsense. You can have a few biscuits and a nice cup of tea.'

'Sorry,' Fliss said, and turning on her heel, she fled back to the loo and retched again.

When she straightened up and turned round, Meg was watching her thoughtfully.

'I don't suppose…'

'What?'

'Could you be pregnant?'

'Pregnant?' Fliss exclaimed, astonished. 'Don't be ridiculous! I'm on the Pill.'

'And what about the bug? Did you take any extra precautions then?'

She opened her mouth to say she hadn't had to, and shut it again. The bug had been just over six weeks ago, just before she'd met Tom.

Just before they'd made love for the first time in her shower at the little house, without thought for the consequences. Two days before, in fact.

Bingo.

'Oh, damn,' she said with feeling.

'Go and do a test.'

She splashed her face with water and glared at Meg in the mirror. 'I can't be pregnant. That's ridiculous.'

'Hmm,' Meg said, and walked out. Less than a minute later she was back, the test in hand, and she shooed Fliss into the loo.

'Oh, damn,' she said again, emerging a minute or two later with the incriminating evidence.

Meg peered at the little stick. 'Positive. Oh, bugger,' she said with her usual candour. 'So, whose is it?'

Fliss looked away, the full enormity of it just beginning to sink in.

'Um—just a guy I know,' she said. She couldn't tell Meg before she told Tom—and telling Tom was something she really, really didn't want to do, now she thought about it.

Five kids. Oh, great. He was going to be so thrilled.

Well, she wasn't exactly overjoyed herself.

'I need to get back to work,' Meg said, looking at her worriedly. 'You go and have a sit-down and something to eat, even if it's just a dry cracker or something. I'll come and see you in a minute—and don't imagine for a moment that we've reached the end of this conversation, because we haven't. I want to know everything there is to know about this mysterious man you've been hiding up your sleeve.'

Fliss panicked. 'I'm fine. I'll come back to work,' she said hurriedly. 'I can't just go and sit in a heap. Anyway, I'm feeling better now.'

She was—more or less—and she needed to keep busy so Meg didn't have a chance to interrogate her. She found herself engineered towards the easy tasks, though, and suspected Meg's involvement in that.

'I thought I was the sister and you were the staff nurse,' she grumbled gently, but Meg just grinned.

'Get over it,' she advised, and swished into a cubicle, leaving Fliss to take the next patient.

It was a simple splinter, a sliver of wood deeply embedded in a child's thumb, and she numbed the skin, pulled the splinter out and dressed the wound before sending him off with the splinter taped to a piece of paper so he could show it off to his friends.

Nice little kid, she thought, and then realised she might be having a son. Or a daughter. But one or the other, definitely.

A child.

Good grief. Suddenly it didn't seem theoretical any more, but somehow real, and therefore much more scary.

And then a woman, Clare Barrett, checked in with a knee injury following a fall down stairs. Her partner helped her hop through to the cubicle, and Fliss made her comfortable on the examination couch while he fussed gently in the background.

'She's having a baby,' he said, and Fliss felt her heart lurch. He looked so proud, really chuffed with himself, and try as she might she couldn't imagine that expression on Tom's face in a million years, not under these circumstances anyway.

'So how exactly did it happen?' she asked, focussing on the patient and putting her own worries aside for now.

'It's so stupid, I can't believe I did it,' Clare said. 'I've been going up and down the same stairs for two years, but I was rushing to the phone. I'd just done a pregnancy test, and I had to tell my husband and my mum—I was so excited, and then the next thing I knew I was at the bottom of the stairs. Idiot. I felt so silly.'

'It was still the first thing she told me when she rang,' Paul said. '"I'm pregnant"—followed by "and I've fallen downstairs".'

Fliss found a smile from somewhere. 'Well, congratulations on the baby, anyway,' she said. 'I take it it was planned?'

'Oh, yes. We've been trying for months. My mum's going to be so pleased—well, not about the knee. Do you think it's badly damaged?'

'I can't say. I'll get a doctor to look at it for you, but probably not. I won't be a moment.'

She went out, dragged in a deep breath and went to find Nick Baker.

'Can you come and do your party trick?' she said. 'Young woman with a dislocated patella and a very happy partner—they've just found out they're pregnant.'

'There must be something in the water,' Nick said, grinning, and went into the cubicle, leaving her staring open-mouthed at his retreating back. Surely Meg couldn't have told him? She'd kill her! The last thing she needed was for Tom to find out before she had a chance to break the news.

She followed Nick into the cubicle just as he was greeting their patient cheerfully.

'Hi, there, I'm Nick. I gather congratulations are in order.'

'Yes—and I'm really glad I've found out, because I can't have any X-rays, can I? Will it be a problem?'

'Well, we can screen you if necessary to protect the baby, but this looks like a classic dislocation so we may not need to take pictures. Mind if I see?'

He moved the knee slightly, and Clare flinched.

'Have you done this before?'

'Not that I know of, but it has been funny from time to time. Sore for no reason, especially if I twist it. It pops a bit.'

Nick nodded. 'It may be a recurrent problem. It if happens again you'll need referring. Fliss, can you give her some gas and air, please, for pain relief? It'll make you feel a bit better,' he said with a smile.

She took a few breaths, and seemed to relax a little.

'So, when's the baby due?' Nick asked, bending the leg slightly and positioning his fingers ready for the manoeuvre that Clare had no idea was coming.

'January. I'm only just pregnant.'

'Snap,' he said. 'My wife told me this morning that I'm going to be a father again in January.' And across the couch Fliss felt the air whoosh out of her lungs in a silent sigh of relief. Then she met his eyes and saw pride and happiness in them—the same pride and happiness that was reflected in Clare's partner's eyes.

There was a lot of it about suddenly, and it made her want to cry.

'Congratulations,' she said, summoning that elusive smile again, and he grinned.

'Thank you. It's going to be a busy month in Maternity. You need to look out for her, Clare. Her name's Sally—Sally Baker.'

'I will—Oh!'

She gasped with pain, her eyes widening, and then she slumped back against the backrest and laughed weakly.

'Oh, that was so sly!'

Nick tutted and wiggled her patella gently, checking that it was properly back in place. 'I don't know, such gratitude. Just say, ''Thank you, Nick'',' he teased, and she laughed again.

'Thank you, Nick,' she said dutifully. 'Oh, that feels much better.'

'We aim to please. I'll get Fliss here to strap it up for you and you should be fine in a few weeks. Just take it easy on the stairs, and do your celebrating lying down.'

'Oh, we'll do that, too,' Paul said, and Nick gave a surprised cough of laughter.

'I didn't exactly mean that, but whatever,' he said, scrubbing his hand through his hair, and Clare chuckled.

'You've embarrassed him, Paul,' she said.

'I think I'm old enough to deal with it,' Nick replied, smiling at them both. 'You take care, now.'

'Thank you, Nick,' they both said, and Fliss busied herself with strapping up Clare's leg and giving her instructions, trying not to think about Tom's likely reaction to the news.

There wasn't going to be much celebrating there, lying down or otherwise, she thought heavily. Just another baby he didn't want.

And the really sad thing was, she didn't know if she did either.

Tom could tell the moment she opened the door that there was something wrong. She'd never been able to hide anything from him, and the look in her eyes made his blood run cold.

'What is it?' he asked without preamble, but nothing could have prepared him for her equally blunt response.

'I'm pregnant.'

He felt the blood drain from his head, roaring in his ears, and he reached out for the doorframe for support, groping blindly until his fingers encountered something firm, something solid, something he could hang onto.

Something real.

'What?' he whispered hoarsely. 'Felicity— how?'

She laughed without humour and walked away. 'The usual way, I imagine. I'd had a bug. I didn't think about it—I'd never had to. I wasn't in a relationship, I hadn't been for years, I'm never sick—it's just not something I thought about.'

'And since then? That was weeks ago. Surely you would have known before now.'

She shrugged. 'Not really. I've had a period—just a light one, maybe lighter than usual, but only the sort you get on the Pill. It's not really the same. I didn't think anything of it until today, when I was sick.'

'So...when...um, when is it...?'

'When's it due? January. January the tenth.'

He closed his eyes. 'That's Catherine's birthday. What a hell of a present. Another kid brother or sister to babysit.'

'Not necessarily,' she said, and he felt a shiver of dread. Not this fight again. She couldn't get rid of it, he wouldn't let her! He hadn't let Jane, he wouldn't let Felicity.

'What do you mean?' he asked, just for clarity.

She shrugged. 'Only that she might not have to babysit. I'd probably ask my mother.'

His shoulders dropped about six inches with relief, and he groped for understanding. 'So, why your mother, when we've got a resident babysitter and my parents on tap?' he asked, wondering why on earth they were worrying about something so trivial when his world had just come slamming to a halt.

Five kids! *Five!*

'Because we won't be together.'

He stared at her, her words making no sense at all.

'Of course we'll be together. We don't have a choice.'

'Of course we have a choice. What if I don't want to be with you?'

He stared at her, shocked yet again. 'You should have thought of that before you let yourself get pregnant,' he retorted, knowing he was being completely unfair but just broad-sided by this totally unexpected and unwelcome news.

'Oh, you did? You thought, before you made love to me that first time in the shower, that if anything happened you'd be happy to spend the rest of your life with me? Get real, Tom! It wasn't like that. Strictly no strings, remember?'

'Well, there are certainly some strings now,' he said bitterly.

'I know—and it's my fault,' she said, surprising him. 'I should have thought about the bug, should have registered. I was the one saying don't worry. I should have been more certain, thought about it more.'

'And done what?'

'Taken the morning-after pill?'

He scrubbed a hand through his hair and sighed shortly. 'Well, you didn't, and I didn't think either, and you can't take all the blame. I should have thought about it myself. What an idiot. Damn, I need this like I need a hole in the head. Well, there's nothing else for it, we'll have to get married. I'm not having my children brought up out of wedlock—'

'Aren't you?' she cut in sharply. 'I would have thought that was exactly what you were doing—or am I imagining that you and their mother don't live together and aren't married any more?'

'That's different.'

'I don't see how.'

He sat down, his legs suddenly deserting him. 'So what are you suggesting? That we live together?'

'No! You seriously imagine I'd live with you and look after all your kids and not have the security of a marriage certificate? Dream on, Tom. I'll live alone with the baby, or with my mother. I don't know. I've not exactly had time to work it out yet, I only found out at one o'clock.'

He propped his elbows on the table in front of him, and realised he was leaning on the plans of the house.

The house Fliss was project managing through a major restoration. Well, there was no way she could do that and work at the same time, not when she was pregnant. No way at all. It wouldn't be safe for the baby, or fair to her.

'I'll have to get another project manager,' he said blankly, wondering where to start and wishing desperately that he hadn't let her talk him into buying this place, because without her, he had no heart for it.

'I'll talk to Bill and some of the others—see if they know anyone,' she said. 'And...ah... I'll move out. Um...'

And then he stopped thinking about himself, about the children, about the house, and thought about Felicity, and the impact this would have on her life. A far greater impact than it would have on his, even if he were to have the child.

'Do you want me to look after the baby? To have custody?'

'You?' she asked, and she sounded shocked and surprised.

'Why not? I've already got four. One more will hardly show. And at least the house is big enough.'

He stood up abruptly, turning round in time to see the frozen look on her face, her hand curled protectively against her taut, flat abdomen, and he felt the fear inside him lessen.

She would love their child, he realised—love it and cherish it and take wonderfully good care of it. She wouldn't be like Jane, who even now was struggling with the kids after less than a week.

It suddenly dawned on him that he'd have to tell them all, and he felt the panic rising again.

One day at a time, he told himself. It didn't show yet, and they didn't know there was anything between Fliss and himself. He could just tell them Felicity was pregnant, and they'd think it was someone else's. After all, it was far too soon for them to have developed that sort of a relationship, even in this day and age!

He closed his eyes and sighed. If only he'd thought, all those weeks ago, when'd he'd met her—thought about it, talked to her, used protection, instead of forgetting all common sense and being driven by his hormones like an over-grown schoolboy.

'I feel such a fool,' he muttered under his breath.

'Don't blame yourself. It's my fault,' she said, and as he watched, a tear welled up and ran down her face, splashing onto her hand. 'I should have thought about it. I'm sorry. I never meant to do this to you—to any of us.'

He sighed and scrubbed his hands through his hair. 'We're probably both equally to blame,' he said heavily. 'But you need looking after, you can't do this on your own. Marry me, Felicity,' he begged. 'We can make this work.'

She snorted quietly and turned away. 'I don't think so, Tom. We'll manage without you. I've got my mother—she'll help us. God forbid we should be a burden. I don't need to be anybody's hole in the head, and nor does my baby.'

Her bitterness shocked him, made him real-ise just how cruel his words must have sounded.

'Oh, hell, Felicity, I didn't mean it like that.'

'No? That's how it came over, Tom. And I think that's what you meant.'

'No.'

'Yes. You can deny it, reason with me until you're blue in the face, but that's what you said, and it was your gut reaction, and you meant it—and I don't want that coming back to haunt me years down the line. And anyway, what the hell would your other kids make of me turning up in your life with yet another sibling? They don't need it. You said that yourself. You vowed you'd never expose them to any danger of hurt again, but you're talking about it now, and while I wouldn't hurt them for the world, I wouldn't stay with you if it wasn't right for us. And it isn't, so there's no point in starting.'

He felt emotion burn the back of his throat, stinging his eyes, and suddenly he needed to get out of there.

He walked blindly to the door, pulling it open, walking out into the courtyard at the back, through the broken gate, out to the car.

Hell. He couldn't drive like this, he couldn't see, and the last thing he needed was her following him.

But she didn't, to his relief, and he sat in the car and stared blindly ahead and waited for the nausea and pain to recede.

Not because she was pregnant, although the shock of that was still echoing through his body, but because she'd been so adamant that she wouldn't marry him, because it wouldn't work.

And suddenly, out of the blue, he realised he wanted it to work. Wanted her in his life, her and the baby, here, in his house, with all of them together, but it just wasn't going to happen.

'Oh, damn,' he said softly.

How on earth could he have let her get pregnant? After Catherine, and then years later the twins, clever money would have learned a few lessons, but not him. Oh, no. He still kept his brains in his boxers, apparently.

And now there was going to be another child, another little Whittaker to worry about

and look after and bring up—because, whatever he'd said to Felicity, whatever his knee-
jerk reaction had been, there was no way he
was staying out of his child's life or letting her
bring it up alone.

No way at all.

Fliss watched him out of the bedroom window,
her heart breaking.

She'd always known he didn't want to get
involved with another woman, but until he'd
talked about needing it like a hole in the head,
she'd had no idea how much he hadn't wanted
another child. Or was it her he didn't want?

Both, probably. Well, she knew he didn't
want to get tied down by a relationship, he'd
said so on that first fateful occasion, before any
of this had started, so it wasn't that he hadn't
warned her. But a hole in the head? That was
harsh.

He was sitting in the car. She couldn't see
him, and she had no idea what he was doing,
but she couldn't go out there and talk to him.

He'd said all there was to say, and so had she, at least for now.

'Oh, baby, what are we going to do?' she said, and turning her back to the window, she slid down the wall until she was sitting on the floor, knees drawn up, her chin resting on her folded arms.

She stayed there like that for an age, until she heard his car start up and drive away, and then eventually she dragged herself to her feet and went through to the kitchen. She needed to eat, although the idea had absolutely no appeal, and she had work to do before the builders came in the morning.

There were decisions to make about the windows, and she needed to talk it over with Tom, but that would have to keep. She'd have to find him another project manager as well, since he seemed to want her off the job.

Probably a good idea, but it was surprising how much it hurt. Not as much, though, as it would hurt building a home for him and his children—his other children—in the house she'd always dreamed of living in, with his child growing inside her day by day.

No, he was right, she'd have to hand the project over to someone else, if she could find anyone.

For now, though, she had things to do. There was more than enough to keep her going for the rest of the evening, just sorting out what order things were to be done in and contacting the various tradesmen.

And the busier she was, the less time she'd have to dwell on Tom's unwelcoming reaction to her news and where on earth she went from here…

'Tom?'

'Hi.' He threw his mother a vague smile and slumped down at the kitchen table, fiddling absently with the sugar bowl. 'You all right?'

'Fine—but why are you home? I thought you were going to eat with Felicity and talk through the house?'

His smile was wry and twisted, he could feel it, and he looked away. 'I was—but she dropped a bit of a bombshell on me. She's pregnant.'

'Oh!' His mother lowered herself into the chair opposite, and he could feel her eyes boring into him. 'Oh, dear.'

'Yes, oh, dear,' he said lightly. 'Bit of a disaster, really. I'll have to find another project manager.'

'Oh. Will you? What a shame. Can't she carry on?'

He suppressed the urge to laugh hysterically. 'Well, I suppose she could, but she's already working at the hospital. It would be too much for her.'

'And she wants to give up? What a pity. She seemed to have so many good ideas, and she was so lovely. I rather hoped—but, no, if she's having a baby, I suppose she's not as single as you'd thought. Oh, Tom, I am sorry. Are you all right?'

He tried to meet her eyes, but she was his mother. She'd known him far too long. He looked away. 'Of course I'm all right. Why wouldn't I be?'

'Because you'd fallen for her?'

'Don't be silly, Mum. I've got more sense.'

'If you say so, dear. But where will she live? Is she still with the baby's father? Can't she live in his house?'

She *is* living in his house, he could have said, but that would have opened a whole new can of worms that he really, really didn't want to get into, not tonight, not ever.

Although he knew he'd have to at some point—but when? The kids would have to know. There were all sorts of issues—custody issues, visitation rights and so on—and that was if he didn't manage to talk her into living with them!

Well, he hadn't given up on that one yet. He'd handled it badly. Badly? Try horrifically. But he'd talk to her tomorrow, ask her to carry on with the house. That was the best thing. Keep her involved with the family, work on her, break down her resolve.

Woo her.

Always assuming she didn't tell him to go to hell.

Goodness knows, he deserved it.

CHAPTER EIGHT

'FLISS, we need to talk.'

She froze for a second with her back to him, her heart sinking. She really, really didn't want to talk to him.

'Is there anything to say?'

She heard Tom's exasperated sigh, heard the sound of him scrubbing his hands through his hair the way he did when things got too much for him. She almost felt sorry for him.

Almost.

'Of course there's something to say—there's lots to say. I just don't quite know where to start.'

'How about "sorry"?' she suggested.

Another sigh, this one quieter, the pause longer. Taking a steadying breath, she turned round and met his eyes, and was shocked by the pain in them. Pain, and remorse.

Good. About time.

'It just seems so inadequate,' he said, his voice rough with emotion. 'I never meant— I know how much the things I said must have hurt you.'

'Do you?' she said bitterly, feeling the hurt rising up again like bile. 'Are you sure you have any idea?'

Another sigh, another assault on his hair, the frustrated stabbing of his fingers illustrating only too clearly how deeply this was affecting him, but was that only because he had no control over it?

She sighed herself this time, and shook her head. 'Not here, Tom. Not at work. Later. Come round after work.'

'OK. What time?'

'Seven? I should have eaten by then,' she said, underlining the fact that she wasn't about to kill the fatted calf for him, but he just nodded.

'Seven,' he confirmed, and turning on his heel, he walked away.

There was something oddly defeated in his stride, something that brought a lump to her throat. No. She wouldn't feel sorry for him, she wouldn't...

'You OK?' Meg asked, coming up beside her, and she dredged up a smile.

'Yes. I'm fine. Just coming to terms with it.'

'Tom looked serious. Everything all right?'

She gave a bitter little laugh. 'Apart from the fact that he's going to lose his project manager? Everything's peachy.'

'Ah. Right. OK. I can see that would be a bit of a worry. So—what are you doing tonight? Fancy a pizza and a nice, long girly chat?'

There was nothing Fliss fancied less—apart from the forthcoming conversation with Tom—but she couldn't tell Meg that. 'Don't think I'm up to pizza,' she said truthfully, 'and anyway, Tom and I have a meeting to talk about the house.'

That last was less truthful, of course, but she wasn't giving her friend any more details than she absolutely had to. Meg was a darling, the salt of the earth, but she was insatiably curious and just now Fliss could do without her curiosity. She had a way of getting information out of people without them being aware of it, and there was no way Fliss was going to give her the chance!

'You won't get away with that for ever,' Meg told her, obviously seeing straight through her excuse, and Fliss felt herself colour slightly.

'It really isn't an excuse—and I will talk to you. Just not yet, OK? I need a bit of time.'

Meg studied her for a second, then hugged her briefly and slapped a set of notes in her hand. 'Here—one for you. It's a nice little industrial injury—some guy's nailed his hand to a plank.'

Fliss winced. 'OK. I'll go and deal with him. Does he come complete with plank?'

'Oh, yes,' Meg told her. 'I've put him in cubicle four, it's bigger!'

She found the man sitting in a wheelchair, the plank with his right hand attached to it resting on the arms and his face a deathly grey.

'Ouch! That was a bit silly,' she said cheerfully. 'Mr Graham, is it?'

'Bob Graham,' he said, and shot her a crooked grin. 'I'd shake hands, but it's a bit awkward.'

She laughed. 'Well, normally we insist, but under the circumstances, we'll let it go. How did you do it, if it's not a stupid question?'

'Air nailer,' he said succinctly. 'I tripped. I had it in my left hand, just about to pass it across to my right to start work, and my knee slipped on a board and I toppled a bit and whacked it down, and bingo. I couldn't believe I'd done it. Just one of those stupid things—going too fast, too much of a hurry.'

'Been there, done that,' Fliss said, understanding only too well. 'I suppose we can just be grateful that you hadn't nailed the board down.'

'Don't,' he said, going even greyer, and Fliss patted his shoulder.

'We'll get you some pain relief and I'll get a doctor to look at you.'

'Ouch!' Nick said, wincing as he passed. 'I knew I hated DIY for a reason.'

'Very funny. Could you have a look for me?' Fliss asked him, but he shook his head.

'Sorry, Fliss, I'm in mid-case. Tom's just finished, I think. I'll get him to come over.'

Just what she didn't need, but this wasn't about her, she reminded herself as he arrived in the cubicle.

'Ouch,' he said, and Bob rolled his eyes.

'Is that all you lot can say?'

Tom grinned and dropped down onto his haunches, peering at the other end of the nail under the board. 'Hmm,' he said thoughtfully, and flicked a glance up at her. 'You're the expert with nails. Got any good ideas?'

'Pain relief first.'

'Sounds good,' Bob chipped in. 'It's hurting like the devil, if I'm honest.'

'Pain relief we can do. We'll numb your whole hand. And then?'

She shrugged. 'I've got a claw hammer in my car, I think. I could tap it back a little, pick up the head and pull it out. Not very sophisticated or high-tech, but probably the quickest and easiest way to do it, and the least traumatic.'

Their patient swallowed, but Tom nodded. 'Sounds good. I'll get started on the pain control, and then you won't feel a thing. You've done it very neatly, you've only hit the fleshy part. The web between the thumb and index finger is full of structures, but most of them are muscles and small blood vessels. The nerves and tendons don't cross it, and there certainly aren't any bones, so hopefully there won't be any lasting damage.'

The reassurance did nothing for Bob. For a moment it seemed that he might well pass out, and Fliss, retrieving her hammer from the car, wondered if she was going to join him. She wasn't normally squeamish, but something about this pregnancy was clearly changing that. She just hoped she could get through the next few minutes without making an idiot of herself.

By the time she got back Tom was about to inject the local anaesthetic to numb the area so they could begin. He wiped the skin with a surgical wipe, located the position of the nerve and slid the needle in, and Bob keeled gently over.

'Whoops,' Fliss said, catching him and easing him back up, and moments later he came round, sweat beading his top lip and his face now totally devoid of colour.

'Did I go?' he asked, and she smiled.

'Just for a second.'

'What a great big girl's blouse,' he said in disgust, and Fliss laughed.

'I don't think that's quite fair. Right, we'll give you a minute to go numb, then, when you're quite happy, we can start.'

'Give me a call when you're ready, I've just got some notes to write up,' Tom said, leaving them, and Fliss settled down at the desk to fill in Bob's notes so far and to keep his mind off the impending procedure.

'So, how come the air nailer? Are you a chippy?'

He nodded. 'Yes—second fix, mostly, for bread and butter jobs, but it's not my first choice. I like doing restoration work, but there isn't much of it about.'

Fliss's ears pricked up. 'Is that right? Can you give me references?'

'Sure—why?'

'Because I'm overseeing the renovation of a huge Victorian house at the moment, and I could do with a decent carpenter on the team. There's a lot of timber restoration to be done— sash windows and the like, restoring the shutters, repairing the pediments round the doors.'

'Sounds like just my thing. I make sash windows—proper ones, exact copies. They aren't cheap,' he warned.

'They never are,' she said with a smile. 'Come and see me, give me a quote. You won't be working for a day or two, and I'm off tomorrow, I'll be there then. And if you can give me the name of anyone I can contact?'

'John Cotton,' he said promptly, and Fliss's eyebrows shot up. She'd heard of John Cotton, and how he'd saved an important listed house from total dereliction.

'You worked on his restoration?'

He nodded. 'I made all the replacement windows and did all the internal joinery. Do you know it?'

'I know of it—and if you did that, I don't need to know any more about you. Come and see me tomorrow, we can have a longer chat.'

Bob nodded. 'I'll do that. Just give me directions.'

'Making a date?' Tom said, coming back in, and Fliss wasn't sure if she'd imagined the proprietorial tone in his voice. She decided to ignore it.

'Absolutely,' she replied calmly. 'Bob's a carpenter. He specialises in restoration work. He's going to come and look at the house tomorrow.'

'Ah.' She could almost hear his ego backtracking. 'Well, excellent. Felicity will fill you in, she knows all about it. I just hand over the money.'

When you aren't telling me that I'm a hole in the head and I've got to marry you, she thought, the hurt rising again, but then put it aside. She had to forget about that while they were working together, both here and at the house—if there was a house for them to work together on. Maybe not. After all, he'd said he'd get a new project manager, so maybe she was being a bit hasty taking anyone else on, but until he found someone else to do the job, the team needed a co-ordinator, and it might as well be her. At least if it was set up right, it would be easier to hand over with a clear conscience.

'Right, Bob, let's have a look at this hand,' Tom said. 'Can you feel it still?'

'I can feel it, but it's like the dentist, you know? Sort of there but not there.'

'Good. Right, who's going to do this?' Tom asked, raising an eyebrow at her, and she shrugged.

'How's your DIY?' she asked, knowing full well what the reply would be, and he just raised an eyebrow.

'Looks like me, then,' she said, more calmly than she felt. They propped the board up on the edge of the desk, she got Tom to lean on it while she tapped the nail firmly back up, and then one quick, clean yank with the claw hammer and it was out.

'Oh, God,' Bob said weakly and keeled over again.

Dropping the hammer, Fliss fled for the loo, resting her face against the cool, tiled wall and taking deep breaths until the nausea receded. By the time she got back, Bob was propped up on the couch, his colour returning slowly, and Tom was examining his hand a little more thoroughly for damage.

Tom glanced up at her, then gave her a closer look. 'You all right?'

'I'll live. Sorry about that, but I guess, unlike you, I'm allowed to be a big girl's blouse,' she said to Bob, and he grinned.

'Got to you, too, did it? I missed that.'

'I wish I had. Right, what are we doing now?'

'Cleaning it up and dressing it. It could do with checking in the morning to make sure the soft tissues don't swell too much, but I think you'll be fine, Bob. We'll give you antibiotics, and Fliss will dress it for you.'

He left, Bob's thanks echoing after him, but she was rooted to the spot.

Fliss. He'd called her Fliss.

She wondered if it had been deliberate, a symbolic severing of any lingering intimacy, or just a slip of the tongue. Somehow she doubted it.

Her name registered with Bob as well, for different reasons, and he tipped his head on one side thoughtfully. 'Are you Fliss Ryman?'

She pulled herself together and forced a smile. 'That's me.'

'I've heard of you. Bill Neills talks about you a lot.'

'You know Bill?'

'Absolutely. We've worked together often. He's a good bloke.'

'I thought I'd heard your name somewhere. Well, that's great, assuming we can afford you. I like to have a team who work well together. I'll get this wrapped up for you, and see you in the morning. Not too early—give me till nine, can you, to get everyone started off?'

'Sure.'

She dressed his hand, gave him a shot of antibiotic and sent him off with his prescription and instructions. 'Do you need the board?' she asked, and he laughed.

'Funny you should say that. I doubt if they'll want it on their floor now, but I might take it home as a trophy.' He chuckled, and took it from her, tucking it under his good arm and heading off towards the pharmacy looking much more cheerful. How he'd be once the pain relief wore off was another question altogether, she thought. No doubt she'd have an update in the morning.

It was a long day. Fliss went home at four, exhausted, and fell into bed for an hour.

Except it turned into three, and she was woken by Tom's knuckles lightly grazing her cheek. The bed dipped under his weight.

'Felicity?' he murmured, and she forced her leaden eyes open and blinked at him, puzzled.

'What time is it?'

'A quarter past seven. I've put the kettle on—I've brought you some herbal teabags.'

'Oh, I can't drink tea,' she said, her throat closing at the thought, but he just smiled.

'I know. They're peppermint, fennel, ginger and cinnamon. I thought they might help with the nausea.'

She sat up, pushing the hair out of her eyes and struggling for a reply. What was the etiquette for such a relationship? Come to that, what was the relationship?

'Thanks,' she said, for want of a better way to start, and he smiled fleetingly.

'Are you OK?'

She nodded. 'Just tired.'

'I'll go and make you a drink. Stay there.'

'No—no, I'll get up. I'm fine.'

After a moment's hesitation he left the room. The door clicked softly shut behind him, and she threw off the quilt and sat up, the world spinning for a moment. Damn. This pregnancy thing was getting to her, she thought, but she had no intention of talking to

Tom about it. She didn't need his pity, and he'd probably use it as a lever to get her to marry him, for the sake of the baby he so badly didn't want.

What a bloody mess, she thought wearily, and tugging on her jeans and a jumper, she slipped her feet into battered old trainers and wandered through to the little room she was using as a kitchen.

'Are you coping all right here?' he asked, looking around with a frown.

'I'm fine—but it's irrelevant anyway, isn't it? I mean, you want me to go, so I'll go. Probably at the weekend.'

He ran his hand round the back of his neck. 'Actually, I don't want you to go. I certainly don't want to make you homeless, but I'm a bit concerned about the lack of creature comforts.'

'I've got plenty of creature comforts,' she told him firmly, and then, less firmly, 'So— what about the house? Do you want me to carry on project managing it for you?'

'Only if you can do it without making yourself ill and exhausted. I just— It seemed to mean so much to you, the house, and everything you said about it just seemed right. Someone else might not see it in the same way.'

So it was only the house. That was what this was all about, getting her to stay on and manage the restoration. Well, she might as well. She'd always loved the house, and as they said in game shows, *I've started so I'll finish.* At least Bob Graham wouldn't be coming to see her tomorrow in vain.

'OK,' she said. 'Let's see how it goes.'

He nodded, sliding her mug across the battered table at her. 'I don't suppose you've eaten?'

She shook her head. 'No. Actually, I'm not hungry.'

'Of course you're not, but you have to eat. I'll cook for you.'

'No, Tom, really,' she protested, but he ignored her, and ten minutes later he put a bowl of plain boiled rice down in front of her, with a few vegetables in soy sauce and honey piled on top, and a little butter dotted around the edge.

She looked at it suspiciously, but after the first forkful she stopped thinking and just ate it, her body ravenous, the flavours just right.

When the last grain of rice was gone, she pushed the plate away and smiled across at him ruefully.

'Thanks,' she said. 'I didn't realise I was that hungry.'

His grin was a little twisted. 'You forget, I've done this before a few times. I know how it works.' He fiddled with his cup for a moment. 'About the house,' he said. 'There are conditions.'

She felt one brow climb up. 'Conditions? I don't know that I do conditions.'

'You do these. You don't go up ladders. You don't do anything yourself, in fact, except supervise from the ground. I don't want to see you running around the scaffolding or checking out the roof, I don't want you carrying anything or working with any hazardous chemicals. I don't want you stripping old lead paint, even with a scraper.'

He was running out of fingers as fast as she was running out of patience.

'I get the point,' she said caustically. 'Don't worry, I won't do anything to harm your precious baby—even if you do want it like you want a hole in the head.'

'Oh, hell,' he said heavily, scrubbing his hands through his hair again. 'I didn't mean it like that. It's just the timing—the kids are still unsettled, their mother really hurt them with her rejection. It's only been three years since she went, and for Catherine and Andrew, it was really deeply wounding. They're great kids, they're coming round, but the twins are starting to wonder why their mummy didn't want them. The last thing they need at this stage is another complication—and don't take offence at being described as a complication, please. This isn't about you or the baby, it's about the kids, and I still have no idea what to tell them.'

'Just tell them I'm pregnant,' she said. 'They'll see soon enough, my tightest jeans are already a bit snug. You don't have to say any more. And I'm sorry I got so uptight about what you said, but, you know, I can feel rejected, too. It's not just your kids.'

'I know. I'm sorry. Sometimes where they're concerned I can't see beyond the end of my nose, but I know it's no excuse.' His smile was forced, and she sensed he was finding this as hard as she was. 'So,' he went on carefully, 'will you stay?'

'If I can. If it works out. It depends how I am, really, but I can't promise not to go up ladders—'

'Then you go.'

There was no reasoning with him, and really he was offering her the easy way out. If she left, she'd only get another house and end up doing a lot of the physical work herself. This way, she only had to supervise, and if she went up the odd ladder when he wasn't looking, how was he going to find out?

'Fine,' she said. 'I won't go up ladders.'

And hopefully he couldn't see straight through the top of the table at the fingers crossed in her lap!

Bob Graham was a great addition to the team. His windows weren't cheap, as he'd said, but they weren't expensive either, and Fliss knew they'd be superb.

In fact, everyone's work was superb, and she was really pleased.

Except, of course, that every time she set foot on a ladder, someone threatened to tell Tom. And he, the rat, had got them all on his side by telling them what she'd not intended to yet—that she was expecting a baby and was to be looked after.

Telling a bunch of macho builders to look after a pregnant woman, of course, virtually guaranteed that she wasn't allowed to lift a finger. She might as well have been bound hand and foot for all she was allowed to do, but on the other hand there were no disputes, no petty squabbles for her to sort out, no slacking on the job or dodgy workmanship.

And things changed in her small area of the house, too. A proper sink unit appeared one day with an instant water heater, so she didn't have to boil the kettle to wash up, and a shower curtain and electric shower over the old bath, so she could wash there properly without having to go round to her mother's.

That in itself was a huge relief, because her mother never wasted an opportunity to ask her about the baby's father, and she wasn't telling anyone that it was Tom's until he'd told his children.

Not even Meg, who turned up one evening in early September with pizza and a bottle of cold fizzy water and dragged Fliss out into the garden to sit under a tree and eat.

The nausea had passed, thank goodness, but that was more than could be said for Meg's curiosity.

'So, come on, you've stalled me long enough. Who is he?' she said, getting straight to the point.

Fliss, feeling much better now, pulled a bit of sticky, stretchy pizza out of the box and caught the strings of cheese with her tongue, stalling furiously. 'None of your business,' she said eventually.

Meg's eyes narrowed, and Fliss looked away, busying herself with the rest of the slice.

'That's the pits. I can't believe you won't tell me! Does he work at the hospital?'

Fliss made a production out of opening the fizzy water, turning the cap too quickly and spraying them both. Meg shrieked and leapt up, laughing, and Fliss thought she might have bought herself some time, but she'd reckoned without her friend's persistence.

'I'll get it out of you one day,' she said in the end, when Fliss obdurately refused to discuss it. 'Want the last slice? Since you're eating for two?'

'And growing like a house. Yes, if you don't want it. I'm starving.'

'So, show me this house, then, if you won't tell me any juicy secrets,' Meg said, resigning herself, and with a sigh of relief Fliss gave her a guided tour.

'Wow. It's huge!'

'He's got four children, don't forget, and his parents are going to be living in the bit I'm using at the moment, and he'll have an au pair as well. They'll be using every inch of it.'

'Good grief! Just imagine all the housework. I wouldn't like to be their au pair!'

They went back outside and strolled around the garden in the dusk, and then Fliss yawned. 'Sorry. It's been a long day.'

'I'll go. I forget how early you're up, even when you're on a late or have a day off, and you're on an early tomorrow, aren't you?'

'No, I'm on at nine,' she corrected. 'Angie's got the day off, I'm covering for her.'

'Hmm. Well, you ought to take it easy, you know. When did you last have a lie-in?'

'Sunday,' she said, not altogether truthfully, but it stopped Meg nagging, and she waved her off, went back inside and put her feet up. Maybe Meg was right, perhaps she should be taking it a bit easier.

She'd finish stripping the fireplace tomorrow night.

*   *   *

'Come on, kids, we're late,' Tom called, checking his watch again.

'I don't want to go back to school,' Abby said petulantly.

'I don't, too,' Michael added.

'I don't either,' Tom corrected automatically.

'You don't go to school,' Abby said, shooting him an accusing look, but he couldn't be bothered to explain.

'Catherine, Andrew, get down here now!' he bellowed up the stairs, and Catherine came clattering down, her hair hanging over her face, Andrew trailing in her wake, bumping his schoolbag down the steps behind him.

'Come on, in the car,' he said. 'Catherine, do something with your hair. Have you got a hair band?'

'Lost it,' she replied, climbing into the front seat and keeping her face turned away.

Make-up, he thought, the light dawning, but he couldn't be bothered to fight with her about it. The school could send her to scrub it off, he didn't have time.

He headed out of the drive, the twins squabbling about something in the background. He blanked them out. Just lately they were always squabbling. It had been a long, tiring summer, punctuated by an unsettling and unhappy week with their mother in the middle, and frankly he'd be glad to see them all settled back into a sensible routine.

The traffic was heavy, of course, because of the start of the new term, and he edged into it and headed in towards town. They reached the ring road, and the traffic started to flow better. He'd just picked up speed, driving along minding his own business with one ear on the kids, when a car shot out of a side turning right in front of him.

'What the—?'

He hit the horn and slammed on the brakes, but there was no time to stop, they were too close. He swerved to avoid it, saw the tree too late, and swore softly.

They clipped the car, slammed into the tree and the airbags deployed with a bang. Then there was another thump, an explosion of excruciating pain and everything went black.

CHAPTER NINE

SHE saw it happen.

From a few cars behind, Fliss saw the little red hatchback pull straight out from the right and cut across the lane of traffic, heard the blast of a horn, the screech of brakes and the tearing, crunching sound of buckling metal as the cars all slid into each other, and then the traffic came to a grinding halt.

'Dear God,' she said under her breath, and cutting the engine, she jumped out of her car and ran to the front of the queue, glancing into the cars as she went.

Shocked occupants were staring blindly ahead, some starting to get out of their cars, others taking a bit longer. No one seemed badly hurt, but the car at the front had mounted the kerb, smashed into a tree and been firmly rammed from behind by a big off-roader.

It was a silver estate car, she couldn't tell what make with all the damage to it, but the horn was blaring and the engine was still running. She opened the door and reached in to turn off the ignition key, and her heart slammed into her throat.

Tom. It was Tom, slumped over the steering-wheel, blood running down the side of his face and dripping all over the now-collapsed airbag, and her imagination went into overdrive.

'Tom?' she said, her heart hammering now behind her ribs, deafening her. 'Tom, talk to me!'

'He's dead!'

She looked up, suddenly realising that the children were all in the car, Catherine in the front seat, her face chalk-white, tears streaking down her cheeks, and Andrew and the twins in the back, their eyes wide with fear.

'It's all right, he's not dead,' she promised, her shaking fingers finding a pulse in the side of his neck. 'Tom, wake up.'

He stirred and gave a fractured groan, and she laid a hand on his shoulder.

'Don't move. Stay there. You need a neck brace.'

'The kids...'

'The kids are fine,' she told him. 'They're all all right, aren't you, kids?'

'It's all right, Daddy,' Catherine said, her voice trembling with reaction. 'It's all right. You just stay there.'

'I'll call an ambulance,' Fliss said, but someone behind her said they'd already done it.

'We need to get him out,' someone else said, but she shook her head.

'No,' she said, and then louder, so everyone could hear, 'Don't move anybody who can't move themselves. Anyone who's hurt should stay where they are until help arrives. Keep out of the way of the traffic, and keep the children safe. The ambulances will be here soon—and can you move right away from the cars with your mobiles? We don't want a spark to send this lot up.'

That last was directed at the man right beside her, and he pulled a guilty face and
headed for the verge. She ducked her head
back inside and smiled reassuringly at the kids.
'You all OK?'

They nodded, but Abby was starting to cry,
and Michael didn't look far behind. Neither,
come to think of it, did Catherine or Andrew,
and she could quite easily have joined in.

'Well done,' she said bracingly. 'Just run
through your bodies, and check everything
feels right. Heads OK? Necks? Arms, legs?
How about your backs and your tummies, with
the seat belts?'

'My chest hurts,' Catherine said. 'From the
seat belt. Why's Daddy's head bleeding so
much?'

'Head wounds always do. It's probably
nothing. Tom, stay still.'

'I'm fine,' he protested, lifting his head a
fraction, but then he groaned and laid it down
again, and Catherine started to cry.

'Don't fall apart, sweetheart,' Fliss said
gently. 'He's all right, and the little ones need

you to reassure them. You go in the back with them and give them a cuddle, and I'll come and sit there and check on your father, OK?'

She nodded, but Fliss could sense her reluctance. While she was moving from the front to the back, Fliss checked quickly to make sure the occupants of the other cars weren't in more trouble than Tom, and having reassured herself, she slid into the passenger seat next to him.

She could feel the waves of resentment coming off Catherine, however, but there was nothing she could do. Turning her attention to Tom, she checked his pulse again and found it was fast but steady.

'I'm all right,' he said, his voice a little slurred round the edges. 'Just a bit dizzy. Think I was out for a moment.'

'How's your neck?'

'Bit sore. I won't move, don't worry. Too much to lose. I know the drill.'

'Good. Just remember it. Anything else hurt?'

'My knee. Must have thumped it on something.'

'Just hang in there, they'll be here soon,' she promised him, her ears straining for the sound of the sirens. Tom's hand reached out, and she took it, heartened by the strength of his grip. She squeezed back, and for a moment they just sat like that, hanging on. Then to her relief she heard the sirens.

'They're coming,' she told him, and he grunted.

The police and ambulance arrived simultaneously, and the children were removed from the car and taken to one side to be checked over. Then a paramedic carefully slipped a neck brace onto Tom, eased him up and started to lift him out.

His agonised groan made her blood run cold, and Catherine gave a little cry and darted back to his side, tears streaming down her face.

'Daddy!' she screamed, but Fliss grabbed her, holding her back out of the way as they manoeuvred him onto a trolley and loaded him into the ambulance. He was still grunting with every breath, and his right leg was at an awkward angle. Broken? Lord, she hoped not. Knees were difficult things.

'What's wrong?' Catherine yelled. 'I want to go with him! Let me go!'

'No. You need to stay with the others, they need you. He's in good hands, Catherine. They'll take you to the hospital and we can check you over. I'm going to follow the ambulance now, I'll see you there in a few minutes.'

'Why can't we come with you?'

She shook her head. 'No. You've just had an accident, you need to be thoroughly checked, have that pain in your chest investigated. Go with the others, please, Catherine. Don't fight me on this.'

She handed her over to the ambulance crew, who were comforting the little ones. Andrew, she noticed, was standing looking lost, and she gave him a quick hug. 'You OK, sport?'

He nodded, hanging onto his control by a thread, she suspected. She didn't push it.

'Good lad. See you at the hospital,' she said, and then running back to her abandoned car as fast as her wobbly legs and pregnancy would allow, she got behind the wheel, pushed her way out into the slowly moving traffic and fretted all the way to the hospital.

By the time she arrived in the unit, they had Tom in Resus and were checking him out.

'I'll take over,' she said to Meg, brushing her aside, and she took his hand.

'How are you?'

'I'm fine. What the hell am I doing in Resus? Isn't that a bit over the top?'

'Getting checked over. What was all the noise about?' she asked, looking down at his leg.

'Bloody knee,' he said succinctly. 'I didn't even realise till they moved me how bad it was.'

'Let's get these threads off you, then, my friend,' Nick said, handing Fliss a pair of scissors. 'Cut away. Let's see what all the fuss is about.'

The fuss was about a kneecap in totally the wrong place.

'Right. We'll have a picture of that, head and C-spine—anything else we need to check?'

'The kids,' Tom said.

'You sound like a stuck record. The kids are being checked over, they're all right.'

'They are, Tom,' Fliss chipped in. 'I've seen them and spoken to them all since they've been out of the car, and they're fine.'

'Go and see them. Are they here yet?'

'I expect so.'

'I want to see them.'

'Not like that, you don't. You're covered in blood from head to foot, you'll terrify them. Let's get you cleaned up and stick that scalp wound back together. Any idea what caused it?'

'Andrew's book, I suspect,' he said drily. 'Something flew through the air, and it's a hardback, so I wouldn't be surprised.'

She parted his hair carefully, and found the still-welling rip in his scalp. 'I'll clean it up and glue it in a minute.'

'Can't you just cover it and get the worst off? They'll be fretting, and I want to see them, too.'

'Later. Pictures first, and once you've got the neck brace off and some of that blood cleaned up, then we'll talk about it.'

The X-rays, fortunately, were clear, but his lips were pressed together in a grim line and she could see his eyes tracking to the light box.

'It's my kneecap, isn't it?'

'It is,' Nick confirmed.

'Damn,' he said softly. 'Well, get on with it, then.'

'OK. You'd better have some Entonox.'

'Just do it, Nick,' he said savagely, but Nick laughed.

'No way, mate. We don't need heroes in here. Gas and air now.' He handed him the mask, waited until he'd had a good few lungfuls, and then took hold of his leg, pressed the heel of his hand firmly on the side of his patella and pushed as he straightened the leg.

The scream turned to a whimper, followed by a stream of words she had no doubt Tom's children had never heard from him, and she propped herself up against the side of the trolley and tried to smile. He had her hand in a death-like grip, and she wasn't sure it would ever work again, but she was gripping back nearly as hard.

'OK,' he said after a minute. 'Can I see the kids now?'

'Nag, nag, nag,' she said gently, but her legs were still like jelly and she found it really hard to walk out and go back to the cubicles to look for the children.

She found them with Meg, and they stared at her, four pairs of grey eyes just exactly like his, three of them afraid, one of them resentful. She swallowed hard. 'He's fine. He wants to see you. I've got to warn you he's covered in blood from the cut on his head, but it isn't serious, and once we've cleaned him up a bit we're going to stick it together.'

'Why did he scream?' Catherine asked unsteadily, distrust in her voice. 'What have they done to him?'

'He'd dislocated his kneecap. One of the doctors just put it back. Knees are very sensitive, they hurt a lot when they're knocked. He'll probably have it strapped up for a few days, but it should be fine. It'll be a lot better now it's back where it should be.'

'Can we see him now?' Andrew asked, and she nodded.

'Are you OK to let them go, Meg?'

Meg nodded. 'Catherine's had a chest X-ray. She may have a cracked sternum, we're waiting for the result. Otherwise she's fine, and the others all seem unscathed. We can't get hold of Tom's parents, though.'

'They'll be walking the dog, they always do at this time,' Catherine said. 'They'll be back soon.'

'Good. Come on, then, come and see your dad, but you'll have to be very gentle. Meg, can you give me a hand? We'll need to lift the little ones up so he can see them. He won't believe they're all right unless he's checked them himself.'

'So this is your gang?' Nick said, grinning easily at them as they all trailed into Resus a moment later. 'Impressive. Be careful not to jump on him,' he warned, but they were almost afraid to go near him. Fliss had picked Abby up, and Meg had Michael in her arms and Andrew by her side, but Catherine hovered beside Tom's head, staring at him with tears streaming down her cheeks.

'You OK, sweetheart?' he murmured, and she nodded, then a huge sob rose in her throat and he lifted his hand and brushed her cheek. 'Is that mascara?' he asked softly, a faint smile on his lips, and she nodded.

'I'm sorry.'

'Doesn't matter. Are you all right?'

'My chest hurts.'

His eyes flicked to Fliss's. 'She'll need an X-ray. She might have some seat-belt trauma.'

'It's been done, we're waiting for the result,' Meg told him firmly. 'Relax, you're the patient here. Trust us, please.'

He nodded. 'Sorry. Andrew, what about you? Are you OK? And my babies?'

One by one, he checked them all, kissing the little ones, holding their hands, while all the time Catherine hovered by his head and stared at him as if she couldn't quite believe he was alive.

Fliss could understand that. Half an hour later, after their grandparents had been contacted and had come and taken them home, and Tom was wheeled up to the orthopaedic ward for observation overnight, she went into the loo, sat down and howled her eyes out.

When she came out, Meg was waiting for her.

'It's his, isn't it?' she said gently, and Fliss couldn't argue any more.

Instead she started to cry again, and Meg just opened her arms and gathered her in.

Once she was more composed they went and got some coffee and took it outside, finding a quiet corner on a low wall where they could talk privately.

'I take it Tom knows?'

Fliss nodded. 'Oh, yes, he knows. He's known from the beginning.'

'And?'

'And what? He told me we'd have to get married.'

'Ah,' Meg said, understanding in her voice. 'Oh, dear. And you love him, of course, and would like to be married to him, but not just because of the baby.'

'I don't know. I thought so, at the beginning, but now, with Catherine so resentful, I don't know if I could cope with it. I don't know if I could face being hated every day.'

'She doesn't hate you.'

'Oh, she does. I'm sure she does. She wants her father's attention all to herself, and I think she suspects something.'

'So—are you still...?'

'What? Having an affair? Hardly. No, Meg, I'm renovating his house by remote control, strictly hands off so I don't hurt the baby, and when it's done, which I've promised them it will be, by Christmas, I'll bow out and go and live with my mother and raise the baby alone. Not ideal, but at least it will be peaceful.'

'But you still love him.'

'Silly, isn't it?' She choked back a fresh wave of tears, blinking to clear them, and Meg patted her hand.

'Come on. Why don't you go and see him, and take the rest of the day off?'

'Because we're short-staffed and I've done nothing today at all yet, and it's after ten.'

'Well, nothing apart from attend an RTA and deal with the victims. I would say that's work.'

She gave Meg a weary smile. 'I suppose so.'

'So go and see him, and reassure yourself that he's all right, and come back when you're ready.'

Fliss shook her head. 'I'll go later. I might ring the ward. I don't want to make a fool of myself, and I'm still feeling a bit shaky.'

She went back in with Meg and threw herself into the fray, and then at the end of her shift she went up to the ward.

'I've come to see Tom Whittaker,' she said, and the staff nurse nodded.

'OK. He's back from Theatre—'

'Theatre?' she repeated, her heart pounding.

'Yes—he had an arthroscopy. He's OK, I think, but you'd better not stay long, he'll be a bit sleepy. He's in the side ward there.'

She nodded and went in, wiping her suddenly damp palms on her tunic. He was asleep, a bruise coming out on his temple, and his right leg was sticking out from the bedclothes. It was heavily bandaged from mid-thigh downwards, and for a moment she just stared at him, content to watch the steady rise and fall of his chest.

She must have made a noise, because he opened his eyes and looked straight at her, and a crooked smile quirked his lips.

'Hi.'

'Hi, yourself. How are you?' she asked, pulling up a chair and perching beside him.

'Knee's bloody sore,' he said frankly, 'and I've got a headache you're welcome to, but apart from that I'm OK. How are the kids?'

'I don't know. Catherine didn't have a crack in her sternum, but I expect she's a bit sore. I haven't seen them since your parents took them home.'

He nodded, then winced.

'Neck ache?'

'Just a bit. I'll go and see an osteopath once I'm out of here. Should be tomorrow, apparently.' He reached out a hand to her, and she took it, squeezing it gently. 'Thanks for looking after us this morning,' he said, his voice gruff. 'I was really glad to hear your voice.'

'Not as glad as I was to hear yours,' she said with a shaky laugh. 'You had me worried there for a moment.'

'Sorry. How's the car?'

She laughed again. 'Pretty rough. You got tailended by an off-roader, and hugging trees is never a good idea. Plus you got hit in the side, of course. I think it might be totalled.'

He snorted softly. 'You could be right. I suppose the police have got all the details?'

'I don't know. I imagine so.'

He closed his eyes and sighed. 'Worry about it later,' he mumbled, and drifted off again. She sat for a few more minutes, then tried to ease her hand away from his, but his grip tightened and so she stayed there, content just to be with him, simply glad that he was alive.

Then behind her she heard Eileen Whittaker's voice, and then Catherine's.

'I don't want to go in there. That interfering witch is in there with him,' she said, and Fliss's heart sank.

Interfering witch? Because she'd told them what to do that morning, she supposed. She leant closer to him.

'Tom? Tom, wake up. Your family are here.'

She removed her hand from his, standing up and smiling at his mother, then letting her eyes settle on Catherine, bracing herself.

'How are you?' she asked.

Catherine glared at her mutinously then looked away. 'Sore,' she said, as if it was utterly obvious and she was talking to a slightly retarded child.

Fliss sighed inwardly. 'I'm sure. I'll leave you alone. How are the others, Mrs Whittaker?'

'All right. I've just brought Catherine for now. David's coming down later with Andrew, but he's got book club until six. We thought the little ones had better not come just yet until we'd seen how he is.'

She nodded. 'I'll let you get on with it. Keep in touch, let me know he gets on. I expect he'll be out tomorrow.'

She went home, passing the accident site and seeing the scarred tree Tom had hit, the traces of glass and bits of broken plastic littering the grass verge. Cold sweat broke out all over her, and instead of going to the house, she turned the other way and went to her mother's.

'Hello, darling,' Helen said, her voice surprised. 'I wasn't expecting you tonight.'

'I know, I'm sorry. I'm just feeling a bit shaky. Tom had a car accident on the way to work.'

'Oh, my goodness! Is he all right? Was he alone?'

'No, he had the kids with him. They're fine, but he had a bash on the head and a dislocated knee. They're keeping him in until tomorrow, I think.'

'Oh, dear. Poor man. Was he brought in?'

She shook her head. 'I was a few cars behind him,' she explained, and filled her mother in on the events of the morning.

'And I don't suppose you've eaten?' her mother tutted, and led her daughter into the kitchen and started ferreting in the fridge.

'Cheese and mushroom omelette?' she suggested, and Fliss smiled tiredly.

'Sounds great, Mum. Thanks.'

'I'll get it, you go and sit down. You look all in.'

She went through to the sitting room without argument, collapsing into her father's old chair and reclining it with a sigh of relief. She was asleep in seconds.

Tom's recovery took a few weeks, but he was back at work within days, of course, limping round the department and giving everyone hell if they tried to suggest he was overdoing it.

'Doctors always make the worst patients,' Meg said in disgust, when she'd had her head bitten off for the third time that day.

Fliss just kept out of it. She'd been called an interfering witch by Catherine, and she had no intention of provoking any further outbursts from any other member of his family, him included.

Instead, she concentrated on keeping her head down at work and getting his house completed before Christmas.

It was coming on. The roof had been done for ages, and one by one Bob Graham had replaced all the rotten windows and restored and repaired the others, and now he was working on the shutters and the panelling in the dining room.

Bill Neills and his son were busy plastering, and the wiring was all completed as far as it could go. The central heating pipes were in, the bathroom plumbing all there in readiness, and Fliss could see the end in sight.

Frankly, it couldn't come quickly enough for her, and she was frustrated by the little she could do to help it on.

One thing she could do, however, was re-store the fireplace in the drawing room that was lurking under layers of paint. Mindful of Tom's concern about the lead content, not to mention her own, she'd sourced some special paste designed for safe removal of old paint, and was steadily, systematically working her way down through the layers.

The tiles were already revealed, and she was thrilled with them. Now she was working on the surround, a beautiful creamy marble, and there was just one more bit to do. She was almost finished, and although it had taken far, far longer than she'd anticipated, at least Tom wasn't hanging around driving her mad and telling her not to do it.

She settled down on the stool, and the baby wriggled into a better position. Automatically her hand went to it, stroking it, soothing it until it had adjusted, and then she started work. She'd just scraped the last trace of paint away and given it a thorough wash down when she heard Tom's footsteps in the hall.

Damn.

She knew it was him because of the limp, and the long pauses as he stopped to study things in passing.

'Fliss?' he called, and she got up from the low stool she'd been using and headed towards the door.

'In here,' she said, wondering if she'd get away with it, but he came in and stopped dead.

'Good grief,' he said faintly. 'Where did that come from? It's gorgeous. When did you buy it?'

'It was there,' she said.

He shook his head. 'No. I would have seen it, it's beautiful.' He went closer, then stopped, bent, picked up the stripper and examined the container. 'Have you been doing this?' he asked, his eyes scouring her, taking in the mucky clothes, the gloves dropped hastily on the floor, the guilt no doubt written all over her face, together with defiance.

'It's safe,' she said flatly. 'I checked. It's my baby, too.'

He stared at her hard for a few seconds longer, then sighed and put it down. 'I hope you're right. And I hope you haven't been overdoing it.'

'No, I haven't.'

'Going to your antenatal checks?'

'Now, why would I do that?' she said sarcastically, and then threw up her hands in defeat. 'Of course I've been going. In fact, I've got a scan tomorrow.'

Something in his face changed, and he swallowed hard. 'May I come?'

Oh, lord.

'Don't you think that will be a bit of a giveaway to the gossips?' she suggested a little desperately, but he just shrugged.

'Maybe. Maybe not. Depends who's doing it.'

'A technician, I expect. I'm under Sam Gregory, but I doubt if he'll be there.'

'I don't think he knows me anyway. If he doesn't ask, I won't volunteer. So—may I?'

She was curiously reluctant. Somehow it seemed so personal, but it was his baby, too, and she was going to have to share it ultimately. It was just that, for now, it was hers and hers alone, and she was enjoying that privacy and closeness.

'OK,' she agreed. 'It's eleven o'clock in the antenatal clinic. I'll meet you there.'

It was amazing.

He'd seen it before with his others, and women were scanned all the time in the department, but this one was his. *His and Felicity's.* That made it very, very different.

'There's the left arm, and the right—look, it's putting its thumb in its mouth. And that's the heart, beating away nice and strongly, and the kidneys are working—look, you can see the bladder emptying. That's good.'

His eyes filled, and he took Felicity's hand in his without thinking.

'Do you want to know what it is?' the technician asked, and he was about to say no when Felicity nodded.

'If you can tell.'

The woman smiled. 'It's a girl,' she said,

and he felt a huge surge of emotion hit him like a wall.

He was going to have a daughter.

Fliss went around for days with a silly smile on her face.

At least now she could plan the baby's layette and start thinking about names, although she was so busy, what with the house and her job, that finding time to do anything for the baby would have to wait.

She started her maternity leave at the end of November, and used the next three weeks to get the house finished off, which involved a lot of bullying, nagging, coaxing and general ankle-biting.

Finally, though, with only a week to go before Christmas and four days before Tom and his family moved in, it was done.

The carpets were down, the curtains were hung and she'd come to say goodbye.

It was beautiful. Fabulous. Everything she could have dreamed of and more, because Tom had thrown money at the project and done everything properly, and it showed.

The kitchen was stunning—hand-built blond oak units, with granite worktops and under-mounted sinks, state-of-the-art built-in appliances and the most stupendous refectory table squatting in the middle of it, just aching for big, boisterous family meals.

The wing his parents were having, the one that had been her home up until a fortnight ago, was now fully refurbished and ready for occupation, and the au pair's quarters, similarly, were ready, as was the rest of the house.

She walked up the back stairs and through the bedrooms, checking the finish, checking the bathrooms, particularly, to make sure that the wonderful honed granite tiles on the walls had been properly grouted and cleaned, and the edges all sealed to stop any water from leaking down behind them.

She went through the bedrooms one by one, mentally ticking them off, each of the children's rooms, and the guest suites, and then went into Tom's room.

It was still empty, but she'd heard his mother talking to him about the bed he'd bought, a huge four-poster, and she could picture it there, with him lying sprawled in it, a lazy smile on his face.

She swallowed hard. She could have been sharing it with him, could have been sharing all of it with him—but at what cost?

No. Let him have his house, wonderful though it was. They would be happy here, they didn't need her, any of them, not really. Tom had got over her, Catherine hated her—and Fliss didn't need that.

She went down the main stairs this time, turning right at the bottom to go into the drawing room. The fireplace was gleaming, a real feature, taking pride of place on the wall opposite Bob's new windows.

Even the garden had been done.

She went over to the fireplace, running her fingers over the silky surface of the marble, remembering the hours it had taken to strip it.

Hours, and love. She'd done it for him, all of it, and now she was going home.

She took one step—or rather, waddle—towards the door, and then the cramp started again.

She'd been ignoring it. She'd had cramps for days, but she'd put it down to overdoing it. Now, as she paused with her hand on the mantelpiece she'd stripped so lovingly, she found she couldn't ignore it any more.

Damn. She didn't need this, it was too early—three weeks too early, to be precise. She was on the point of phoning her mother when she heard the front door open and close, and Tom came in.

'Everything all right?' he said, and then his eyes narrowed. 'Are you OK?'

'I'm fine,' she said, and then the next contraction hit her.

CHAPTER TEN

TOM took one look at Felicity's face and swore softly under his breath.

'When did they start?' he asked, but she ignored him, turning to lean both arms on the mantelpiece, breathing lightly at the top of her chest. Using her exercises, he realised, and his heart sank.

'Yesterday, I suppose,' she said after a minute or so of silence filled only with the sound of her light, rapid breathing.

'Right. In the car, I'm taking you to hospital.'

'Tom, I'm all right.'

'And I'm a fairy. Come on.'

He put an arm round her, steering her out of the room, through the front door and into the car.

'I need to get my things from Mum's,' she said, but then another contraction hit her, and he shook his head.

'No. You're going to hospital now. I'll get your things later.'

She opened her mouth to protest, but gave a gasp of pain instead, and then, after another session of panting, she sighed softly.

'Tom?'

'Uh-huh?'

'About your new car.'

'Mmm.'

'My waters just broke.'

He couldn't help it, the whole thing was suddenly too much for him.

He started to laugh.

He was laughing! She was having her baby, right there in his car, and he was laughing, for heaven's sake, while she trashed his upholstery and fought the urge to push.

'Dammit, it's not funny, Tom—I really am having it now.'

He shot her a quick look, swore again and put his foot down.

'I hope you're not going to keep using that word in front of the baby,' she said snippily, and gasped as another wave of pain hit her, accompanied by a terrible urge to push. 'Tom, hurry up!'

'I'm hurrying up. Any faster and we'll end up with a police escort.'

Which was exactly what did happen, to Fliss's relief. It whisked them past the traffic, into the unloading area in front of Maternity and left them there with a chorus of good wishes.

Huh! She'd give them all the best.

'Why is it the lift's always at the top when you need it?' she complained from her wheelchair, starting to panic now, and he took her round the side and used the theatre lift, arriving at the ward just in time for another contraction.

She slapped his hand away when he tried to help her up onto the bed.

'I can manage. You've done more than enough,' she snapped, crawling onto the bed on all fours and falling against the pillows. 'I hate you, Tom Whittaker, do you know that?' she mumbled. 'You're the pits.'

'Transition, is it?' the midwife said calmly, and Fliss heard Tom giving a potted history of her labour behind her back.

'I am here, you could ask me,' she growled, and then wailed softly as another contraction gripped her.

'The baby's not due for another three weeks,' Tom was saying. 'She's been over-doing it.'

'Are you her partner?' the midwife said.

Tom said, 'Yes, I am.'

Simultaneously, Fliss snapped, 'No, he damn well isn't! He's just the father!'

'I hope you're not going to use that language in front of the baby,' he said virtuously, and she lashed out and caught his arm with the back of her hand.

'Ouch,' he said, chuckling, and then she felt his arm around her, supporting her as she gripped the top rail of the bedhead and pulled herself up to her knees.

She felt the midwife pulling off her clothes, peeling the wet trousers down, examining her, her hands gentle, one of them on the small of her back, rubbing slowly, as Tom's other hand lay on the curve of her belly, stroking it with feather-like strokes, so soothing.

She leant against him. She couldn't help it, she didn't want to need him, but she did. She started to cry, big, rending sobs, and he shushed and rocked her, holding her when the next contraction came and the midwife told her to push, there for her when an amazing force seized her in its grip and took control.

'Tom!' she wailed. 'I can't do this!'

'Yes, you can.'

'No,' she whimpered, totally overwhelmed by the power of this thing that was happening to her. 'It scares me, and it's too early. I'll come back later, I will, in a week or two, but not now, please. I can't cope.'

'It's all right, it's just your body taking over,' he said soothingly. 'It's your heritage, Felicity. You're a woman. Be proud of it. You can do this. Just let your body steer you, and lean on me. I'll hold you.'

And he did, through every terrifying and amazing and exciting second, until she heard the sound of her newborn daughter's cry, and then he lowered her to the bed and put the baby in her arms, and it was as if everything in the world suddenly made sense.

'Is she all right?' she asked worriedly.

The paediatrician was there, materialising from nowhere to check the baby out and listen to her lungs, but from the hearty wails it was obvious that her breathing was fine.

'She's gorgeous. Good size for her dates, and she's lovely and strong. We'll keep a close eye on her, but she looks fine. We'll just have to keep her warm for a day or two, in case her temperature regulation goes a bit funny, but she may get away with it and not need a special cot. Well done, Fliss. Clever girl.'

She felt weak with relief. 'Hello, my darling,' she said softly, and the baby stopped crying and started to nuzzle at her breast.

'Here,' Tom said, and taking the baby's head in his hand, he turned it and pressed it firmly onto her nipple.

Good grief! The power in that tiny mouth, she thought. It made her feel quite lightheaded, just watching her suckle.

Very light-headed, in fact.

Dizzy.

'Tom?' she said faintly. 'I feel weird. Can you take her?'

And then the darkness engulfed her.

'What the hell's happening?' he snapped. 'Her pressure's crashing, she's in shock! She must be haemorrhaging! Do something!'

The midwife hit the crash button, whipped the pillows out from under Felicity's head and peeled back the top sheet. Blood was pooling on the bottom one, and Tom's heart slammed into his throat. Dear God, he couldn't lose her!

All hell broke loose in the next few seconds. A man he vaguely recognised as Sam Gregory appeared in the doorway, took one look and said, 'Get her up to Theatre. Has she had oxytocin?'

'Yes. She hasn't delivered the placenta yet and I can't pull any harder on the cord, she'll prolapse.'

'Right. Let's get her up to Theatre, we can't do anything here. Someone look after that baby, please. Come on, folks, let's go.'

And Tom realised he was holding the baby in his arms, wrapped only in a towel, and he watched in horror as they wheeled Felicity out and ran towards the lift.

'Here, let me have her,' a nursery nurse said gently, and she took the baby from Tom's arms.

'She's premature—she's only thirty-seven weeks,' he said, his eyes following the trolley racing down the corridor. 'Look after her, I'm going with her mother,' he said, and ran after them.

Two hours later, two hours that were the longest of Tom's life, he was sitting by Fliss's bed in Recovery, holding her hand and willing her to live.

He had no idea where the baby was. It didn't matter, she'd be in good hands. Felicity was his immediate concern.

He stroked the hair back from her face, swallowing the huge lump in his throat, but it wouldn't go away. Her mother was there, sitting on the other side of the bed, holding her other hand. Her eyes were closed, her lips moving—in prayer?

Probably. The words were going round in his head, too. Don't let her die. Please save her. I'll do anything you tell me to do, only don't let her die.

Helen stood up stiffly and looked down at him, her eyes, so like Felicity's, full of pain and fear. 'I'm going for a walk. I won't be far away. Call me if there's any change.'

He nodded, hearing the door open and close, his eyes never leaving Felicity's face.

'Wake up, sweetheart,' he pleaded. 'Come on, you can do it. Your baby needs you—dammit, I need you. I love you. You can't do this to me—please, Felicity, wake up. Don't leave me. I can't live without you—'

He broke off, his head falling forwards against the cot sides, her hand lying unmoving in his own.

And then it twitched, squeezed his fingers, and his head jerked up, his eyes flying to her face.

'Tom?' she whispered.

He stood up, his legs like jelly, and bent over her, smoothing the hair back from her face with a trembling hand. 'Felicity?'

'Hi. What happened?'

'You haemorrhaged. The placenta wouldn't detach properly. You had to go to Theatre.'

She nodded, her eyes still slightly glazed. 'How's the baby?'

'I don't know. Fine, I think. Nobody's said anything more, but she was all right.'

'Is Mum here?'

He nodded. 'She's just gone for a walk. I'll get her.'

'Wait—what you were saying…just now. About loving me…'

He swallowed hard, nodded. 'What about it?'

'Did you mean it?'

He laughed, a short, desperate little sound. He tipped his head back, blinking away the tears, struggling for control. After a steadying breath, he looked back down at her, at her drawn, fragile little face, her eyes dark hollows against her pale skin.

'Yes,' he said softly. 'Yes, I meant it.'

'Oh,' she said. 'Can you get Mum, and find out how the baby is?'

Oh? That was it? No reciprocating expressions of love, no lifetime commitment? But what had he expected, after the way he'd treated her, the things he'd said? He swallowed down his disappointment and nodded.

'Of course.' He bent over, pressing his lips to her forehead in a lingering kiss, then straightened up, walked out of the door and slumped against the wall. A sob of relief escaped, and Helen ran up to him, her face frantic.

'No!' she whispered, and he shook his head.

'No, no, she's fine. She's fine, Helen. She's going to be all right. She wants to see you.'

Tom went home late that night, walking into the kitchen and stopping the conversation dead.

His parents, Catherine and Andrew were all seated round the table, and they looked up at him questioningly.

'She's OK. They're both OK.'

His mother got to her feet, walked over and took him in her arms. 'Thank God,' she said softly, and then he let go.

'Dad?'

'I'm all right,' he said, raising his head and dragging in air. He scrubbed the tears from his face with the heels of his hands and gave the children an unsteady smile. 'I'm all right. It's just been a hell of a day.'

'And the baby?' his mother asked.

He felt his smile soften. 'The baby's gorgeous. She's tiny, but she's beautiful and she's doing really well. I've just left her sleeping.'

Catherine looked at him steadily, a new maturity in her eyes. 'She's our sister, isn't she?' she asked, and he couldn't lie—not then, not ever, not about something so amazing and beautiful and wondrous as one of his children.

'Yes, she is.'

'I thought so. When we had the accident—she was funny with you. Possessive. Like she loved you.'

His smiled twisted a little. 'Yeah, well, I don't know about that. We'll see. And now you kids really need to be in bed,' he said, struggling to get back to normality, and as if sensing the turmoil in him, they didn't argue, bless their hearts. They just got up, hugged him, kissed him goodnight and went.

'And you?' his mother said. 'Are you all right, really?'

He shrugged. 'I'll do. I'm really tired. I think I'll turn in. We've got a lot to do in the next few days, with the move.'

'And how do things stand between you and Fliss?'

He gave a strangled laugh, full of all the despair and confusion that was in his heart.

'I have no idea.'

Fliss hardly saw him for the next few days. He was busy moving, of course, and he was still at work, so his visits were few and far between, snatched minutes here and there, but never time to talk, to say the things she needed to hear, for her to say the things she wanted to say.

And his eyes were always for the baby.

Sam Gregory came to see her, and told her that it had been touch and go whether he'd need to do a hysterectomy.

'We got away with it, thankfully, and there's nothing to stop you having as many more perfectly healthy children as you want.'

Nothing except the fact that the man she loved didn't seem to want to talk to her now. He'd said he loved her, but had that just been in the heat of the moment, in the fear of losing her? Now she was all right, he almost seemed to be avoiding her.

No, that was unfair. He wasn't avoiding her. He was just rushed off his feet, and the day before Christmas Eve they moved into the house, so she didn't see him, and the next day she was going home, and he'd be tied up with his family all over Christmas, so she wouldn't see him then.

Her eyes filled, and she blinked them away. Silly. It was just the baby blues. Everybody got them on the fourth day, she'd been warned about it, but she just wanted to curl up in a corner and howl her eyes out.

At least the baby was OK, fine and strong and not suffering at all for her mother's stupidity in overdoing it so much to get the house done on time.

Her mother came to see her that evening, bringing her clothes and the tiny things for the baby, ready for taking her home the following day.

Except her mother didn't come the next day, Tom did, looking tense and uptight and a little distracted.

'Where's my mother?'

'She had to go shopping, to get things for the baby. She asked me to pick you up,' he said, but he avoided her eyes and she felt he was lying for some reason. But what and why?

He dressed the baby, his hands unbelievably gentle and practised, and within moments she was snuggled up in a tiny suit that drowned her, and he was wrapping her in a blanket and tucking her into a portable baby seat, strapping her in firmly, safely.

'What about you?' he asked. 'Can you manage to walk, or do you need a wheelchair?'

'We always take them to the car in a wheelchair,' the nursery nurse said, coming to see them off, and they went down in the lift and Tom brought the car to the door.

'Did your upholstery survive?' Fliss asked, and he laughed.

'Sort of. I had it cleaned, it's OK.'

'I'm sorry.'

'Don't worry. It doesn't matter.'

He settled her in the seat, clipped the baby into the seat behind her and then slid behind the wheel. 'All set?'

She nodded. She was ready to go home, inexplicably tired and emotional, and she just wanted to crawl into her bed in her old bedroom at home and hide.

But they didn't go there. Instead, he turned into the drive of the Red House, and she shot him a puzzled glance.

'Tom?'

He stared straight ahead. 'There's something not quite right at the house, something that needs your attention. I wondered if you could just check it out, so we can sort it before Christmas.'

The house. Always the house, she thought, on the verge of tears. She'd nearly lost her baby because of the blasted house.

'What sort of something?'

'It just feels cold,' he said, but there was something odd about his voice, and a muscle was working in his jaw.

He pulled up by the front door on the freshly raked gravel sweep, and she could see lights blazing in the drawing room.

The front door opened, and his mother came out.

'Hello, Fliss, dear. How are you?'

Eileen kissed her cheek, opened the rear door and unclipped the baby. 'I'll just take her in out of the cold,' she said, and whisked her away before Fliss could say a word.

'Come on,' Tom said, tucking his hand under her elbow and helping her from the car, and then he led her slowly in through the front door.

'It feels lovely and warm,' she said, puzzled, and he smiled, his mouth crooked, his eyes somehow…afraid?

'It does now,' he said quietly. 'Now you're here. Come in.'

He opened the drawing-room door, and she stopped on the threshold and took it all in, everything, exactly as she'd described it down to the last detail.

The tree, a huge one, filled the corner, soaring to the ceiling, the tiny white fairy lights making the corner glow. Presents were piled on the floor at its foot, and over the pictures and around the windows were hung holly and ivy and mistletoe. She'd bet her last penny they were from the garden.

The fire was blazing, crackling away behind a sturdy fireguard to keep it safe, and he led her to one of the sofas grouped around it and sat her down, then went over to the tree and slipped something from under it into his pocket.

'Tom, what are you doing?' she asked, but she didn't have to wait long.

He came back to her, hunkering down in front of her, and took her hand in his. His fingers were cold, and for a moment she thought she felt them tremble, then he cleared his throat and looked up and met her eyes.

'I want to say something—so many things, really, that I don't know quite where to start, but maybe I should start with saying sorry again. You see, I've lied to you—to you, and to myself, right from the very beginning, when I told you that I didn't want to get involved with you. I mean, I didn't, it was a crazy idea, and the timing was lousy, but I fell in love with you the moment I set eyes on you in the department that first day, and I've been lying to myself and to you about it ever since.'

He loved her. He did, he really loved her! She opened her mouth to speak, but he laid a finger on her lips and shook his head.

'No,' he said. 'Let me say it, please, get it out of the way, then you can talk all you want, or go, or whatever. Just let me say this, because I've messed it up once well and truly, and I don't want to mess it up again.'

He looked down at their hands, and she felt his fingers tighten. 'I've wanted to be with you from the very first moment I saw you. I just couldn't see any way to achieve it, though, except the way we had, and I know it was less than satisfactory but it meant we could be together and nobody was being hurt. Nobody except you, of course, and me, but we were adults. We could handle it, the kids couldn't, or so I thought.

'But I wanted more. I wanted everything, and when you said you were pregnant—well, it was a hell of a way to force the issue, but it was like fate making the decision for us.'

'Only I said no.'

'You said no. But to be fair, I didn't exactly put it well, and once I'd said all those things, there didn't seem to be any way back. But I realised then how much I love you, and how deeply I'd hurt you, and I didn't know what to do, which way to turn. So I did what I do best.

I did nothing. I thought I'd wait, and time would sort it out, and then you nearly died...'

His voice broke, and she laid her other hand over his and squeezed. 'But I didn't.'

'No. No, you didn't. Fate gave me one last chance, and I hope to God it's not too late, because I've fallen in love with you so hard and so far that I'll never get out alive.' He swallowed, then met her eyes again, and she could see all the way down to his soul.

His dear, tortured, beloved soul, so precious to her.

He shifted, so he was on one knee—the left one, the one he hadn't injured. 'Marry me, Felicity,' he said gruffly. 'I know it's a hell of a lot to ask of you, and I know you think Catherine hates you, but she doesn't, and she needs a friend. She's got a mother, she doesn't need another one, but she could do with someone a little closer in age than her grandmother to bounce ideas off, and so could Andrew, and the little ones would be playmates for the baby. And as for me...'

'As for you?' she prompted.

'You're my other half. I need you, Felicity. I love you, and I want to grow old with you and our children, and spend the rest of my life with you. I can live without you, if I have to, but nothing would ever be the same again. There'd be no colour, no laughter, no joy in anything without you by my side. Say you'll marry me—please?'

She couldn't. She was so choked with emotion, she couldn't find the words. She just shook her head mutely, and bit her lips, and felt the tears well in her eyes.

'Yes,' she said finally, 'oh, yes, please,' and threw herself into his arms.

A cheer went up, and she heard the family come in, a great eruption of excited chatter and laughter, but she was busy, because Tom was kissing her as if he'd never let her go.

He kissed her everywhere, his lips smothering her face, her hair, her mouth, and she lifted her hand to his cheek and it came away drenched with tears, but whether hers or his she couldn't tell.

Probably both.

'I love you,' he said finally, lifting his head to stare down into her eyes. 'And I will do everything I can to make your life happy.'

'You don't have to do a thing,' she said, smiling at him through her tears. 'Just be there for me.'

'Or here, even,' he said softly. 'In our house—our home.'

'That sounds wonderful,' she said.

'So does it fit?' Andrew said.

'Does what fit?' Michael asked.

'Fit?' Fliss said, but Tom just gave a rueful shake of his head.

'I haven't even got around to it.' He pulled a little box out of his pocket and gave it to her, and she opened it, gasping.

'Tom! Oh, Tom, it's beautiful!'

Her fingers traced the ring, a simple band with a row of flawless square-cut diamonds set end to end within the gold.

'I didn't think there was any point in getting you anything which stuck out, because I want you to wear it all the time, and I know you, you'll be plumbing and ripping out kitchens and doing something silly and catching it on things and hurting yourself.'

She laughed. 'No plumbing, I promise,' she said.

'What, not even if we spring a leak?'

'Well, maybe then,' she relented, and held out her hand. 'Put it on,' she said, and he lifted it out of the box and slid it slowly over her knuckle.

'It fits,' the children chorused, but Tom didn't take his eyes off hers.

'With this ring, I thee wed,' he murmured softly, and kissed her...

MEDICAL ROMANCE™

Large Print

Titles for the next six months...

July

THE FIREFIGHTER'S BABY	Alison Roberts
UNDERCOVER DOCTOR	Lucy Clark
AIRBORNE EMERGENCY	Olivia Gates
OUTBACK DOCTOR IN DANGER	Emily Forbes

August

EMERGENCY AT INGLEWOOD	Alison Roberts
A VERY SPECIAL MIDWIFE	Gill Sanderson
THE GP'S VALENTINE PROPOSAL	Jessica Matthews
THE DOCTORS' BABY BOND	Abigail Gordon

September

HIS LONGED-FOR BABY	Josie Metcalfe
EMERGENCY:	
A MARRIAGE WORTH KEEPING	Carol Marinelli
THE GREEK DOCTOR'S RESCUE	Meredith Webber
THE CONSULTANT'S SECRET SON	Joanna Neil

MILLS & BOON®

Live the emotion

0605 LP 2P P1 Medical

MEDICAL ROMANCE™

Large Print

October

THE DOCTOR'S RESCUE MISSION Marion Lennox
THE LATIN SURGEON Laura MacDonald
DR CUSACK'S SECRET SON Lucy Clark
HER SURGEON BOSS Abigail Gordon

November

HER EMERGENCY KNIGHT Alison Roberts
THE DOCTOR'S FIRE RESCUE Lilian Darcy
A VERY SPECIAL BABY Margaret Barker
THE CHILDREN'S HEART SURGEON Meredith Webber

December

THE DOCTOR'S SPECIAL TOUCH Marion Lennox
CRISIS AT KATOOMBA HOSPITAL Lucy Clark
THEIR VERY SPECIAL MARRIAGE Kate Hardy
THE HEART SURGEON'S PROPOSAL Meredith Webber

MILLS & BOON®

Live the emotion

0605 LP 2P P2 Medical